Innvitation to Murder

A Maddie Brooke Mystery

Nancy M. Wade

INNVITATION TO MURDER

Published in the United States

GARNAN Enterprises, LLC of Ohio.

Copyright 2024 by Nancy M. Wade

All Rights Reserved.

ISBN – 979-8988552277

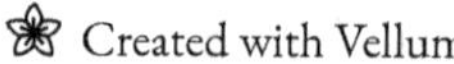 Created with Vellum

Foreword

Welcome to "Innvitation to Murder," a captivating cozy mystery set at the picturesque Magnolia Blossom Inn, nestled in the charming town of Clarkstown near the gateway to the Shenandoah Valley just outside Charlottesville, VA.

Come sit a spell and enjoy the peaceful Magnolia Blossom Inn. Don't pay no mind to the elderly woman that floats on by – that's just Grannie's ghost come to greet her guests along with her dog, Luke.

Twenty-two-year-old Maddie Brooke inherits her grandmother's inn plus the mystery of how Grannie died. When another guest at the inn is found dead, Maddie must face real dangers from this world and beyond to solve the crime.

Can she find the killer in time to prevent the loss of her beloved home? Maddie seeks help from the handsome Yankee detective, Allen Crawford, and her close college friends Lionel and Lily to solve the crime.

Also by Nancy M. Wade

Contents

Cast of Characters

- **Polly A. (nee Stewart) Brooke** – Grannie, married Charles Brooke with southern roots dating back before Civil War.
- **Madison Leigh Brooke (Maddie)**- 22 year old granddaughter of Polly, graduate of UVA in Charlottesville, a history major with a nose for research and investigation.
- **David James Brooke** – Maddie's father, a sea captain who prefers the ocean blue to family life.
- **Thomas Borden** – long time employee of the Magnolia Blossom B&B; he is chef and handyman at the inn.
- **Detective Allen Crawford** – a Philadelphia Yankee who's joined the Charlottesville police force; he solves crime while dazzling the local female population.
- **Lionel Hogan** – Maddie's school friend. Lionel is a wiz with computers; works as an I.T. forensic security analyst.
- **Dr. Lily Chung** – Maddie's former roommate at UVA, Lily is an intern at the UVA Medical Center
- **Bobbie Jo Taylor** – Maddie's cousin on her mother's side, is a spoiled brat used to getting her own way with a smile and flirtatious look. She studies art at the university.

- **Attorney Wallace Jackson** – the Brooke family retainer and old friend of Charles and Polly.
- **Dr. Wilbur Houser** – southern gentleman, country doctor who has known Polly since they were both young.
- **Chief Bill Barlow** – runs the detective division of Charlottesville PD; resents Crawford as a know it all Yankee
- **Attorney Lee Warner** – counsel for the heritage center
- **Sean O'Reilly** – an Irish exchange student studying at UVA and staying at the bed and breakfast for the summer.
- **Noah Foster** – handsome, summer student resident from the UVA
- **Prissy** - the black and white tuxedo cat living in the barn.
- **Luke** – Grannie's overly-protective German shepherd
- **Folks of Clarkstown**
- **Guests of Magnolia Blossom Inn**

Prologue

The sun glinted off the metal colander that I carried. I heard a slight noise as I neared the barn entrance. I paused, listened, then called out.

"Grannie? Are you in here?"

Dust motes swirled in the shaft of light coming through the open barn door. Prissy the cat screeched and Luke barked from somewhere in the depths of the large barn. My eyes took a second to adjust to the interior shadows then widened at the sight of Grannie lying on the straw strewn floor.

Dropping the colander, it clattered and rolled on the cement surface. I rushed to my grandmother's side and dropped to my knees. She lay unmoving, yet I saw no signs of blood or injuries. Oh my God! What happened?

I grabbed my cell phone from my back pocket. With shaking fingers I punched in 9-1-1 and tried to sound coherent as I gave the dispatcher my information.

"Please hurry! She needs help!"

Cradling her head in my lap, I waited anxiously. Tears blurred my eyes as Doctor Houser hurried to my side.

Chapter One

Grannie

Copious tears rolled down my cheeks. I brushed them away with an angry swipe of the back of my hand. Staring at the tiny silver-haired woman lying serenely in the coffin before me, I couldn't believe she was gone. How could God be so cruel to take away the only maternal love and care I'd ever known? What was I to do? How could I think of the future without my beloved grandmother?

My father stood silently by my side as lines of well-meaning towns-folk filed past, extending their condolences. Shamefully, I only thought of myself today, my loss, yet the strange man beside me also grieved the passing of his mother. It was selfish of me. Vowing to do better, I promised to make an effort to get to know my paternal parent now that he had returned home. I had to; there was just the two of us now.

Shuttering my thoughts, I smiled at my approaching school friend as he pressed his ebony hand against my arm. Lionel Hogan and I had shared several classes at the University of Virginia during the past three years. I wouldn't have completed two geology courses without Lionel's help during my sophomore year. He's a scientific genius. Fortune smiled on me when he came into my life and offered his friendship.

"Maddie. How're you holding up?" asked Lionel. His large brown eyes smiled tenderly.

Lionel's solicitation was almost my undoing. I blinked back a fresh wave of tears as I nodded. "Thank you for coming," I said. "You'll stay for the luncheon?"

"Of course. I think Lily will be here soon. She had to finish her shift at the hospital."

"I hope she isn't taking time away from work; I know how short-handed they are at the hospital. Still ... I've got to talk to Lily. Maybe she can make sense out of this." I waved my hand toward the casket and my beloved grandmother. "I was just with her that morning, Lionel. She wasn't ill. How could she die so suddenly?" I shook my head and swallowed to gain a level of composure.

Lionel squeezed my hand again. "I don't know. Hey, I'll be right over there if you need me." He pointed to a cluster of chairs along the back wall.

"Okay. Thanks."

Quiet voices murmured in conversation as people waited solemnly for the service to begin. I moved to stand next to the coffin and fingered the sprigs of lily of the valley lying across my grandmother's crossed hands. The delicate scent filled my nostrils and triggered memories of the vibrant, laughing woman that so loved the tiny bell-like blooms. Grannie always said no expensive flowers for her. She preferred the natural blooms and wildflowers that dotted the landscape and filled the gardens of her home outside Clarkstown.

Leaning forward, I kissed her cold, smooth cheek. A teardrop fell upon her face. *Oh Grannie ... how will I manage without you?* Seeing the minister enter the room, I returned to my seat next to my father.

Reverend Moore stepped to the front of the visitation room. He paused and said a silent prayer next to the deceased then turned to face Polly's family and friends that had gathered in the large space.

My mind drifted as I listened to the soft piano music playing in the background. The minister's words washed over me.

"Thank you all for being here today to honor the life of Polly Ann Brooke. She was a remarkable woman, known for her warmth, kindness, and the love she shared with everyone she met. As we gather to remember her, let us take comfort in the memories we shared with her and the legacy she leaves behind."

Reverend Moore gestured toward a large photo of Polly near the foot of the coffin. My eyes were drawn to it and a smile curled my lips as I studied the picture and recalled that warm summer day. The photographer had captured her laughing and hugging me as a young, blonde-haired child while her German shepherd, Luke, romped in a field of wildflowers.

"Polly was not just a mother to David or a grandmother to Madison, she was a friend. A pillar of our Clarkstown community. Her bed and breakfast inn wasn't just a place to stay; it was a sanctuary for travelers, a home away from home. She welcomed strangers with open arms, treating them like family from the moment they crossed her threshold," the minister continued.

"Polly Brooke's hospitality was matched only by her generosity. She had a knack for seeing the good in people and helping them find it within themselves. Her legacy will live on in the countless lives she touched, the stories shared, and the memories cherished. Let us take solace knowing that her spirit will forever remain with us, guiding us with her love and wisdom. Though she may be gone from our sight, Polly will never be absent from our hearts.

Reverend Moore concluded the service with a moment of silence, broken only by the soft sobbing of a few mourners or by spoken memories of Polly's kindness and friendship. Neighbors shared anecdotes and stories, celebrating her life, as they slowly dispersed to join the luncheon hosted by the church women's club.

I stood next to her body, reluctant to leave and dreading the moment when her coffin would be closed and she'd be forever gone from my sight.

A hand touched my shoulder awkwardly and I looked over at the man who had chosen the sea over his family. His tendered comfort felt foreign and forced; he must have thought so too as he dropped the hand to his side.

Glancing around the room, I realized we were alone. I faced him and studied the weathered face, sunburnt skin with lines flaring out from the corners of his narrowed blue eyes. Eyes the same color as my own.

"I don't know what to say. You've only been home three times in the last fifteen years. I don't know you," I said in a flat voice that was emotionally drained.

"I'm sorry Maddie. I should have been here for you, but, well ... your Grannie took good care of you. After your mother's death, I didn't know what to do with a seven-year-old girl. I had to earn a living and the sea was all I knew. Guess I thought that by sending money home all the time, that was enough. You got to go to college on my hard earnings; I tried to do right by you."

He defended himself and his actions as if they were enough to fulfill his parental duties. He never understood that a lonely child needed a shoulder to cry on or a pair of arms to shelter within, a smile of encouragement, or a kiss goodnight.

"I know you did what you thought was right, but it wasn't enough. You've got to realize, that for me, Grannie was the only parent I had and now she's gone." I sobbed and turned, running out of the room. My father stood alone, a stricken expression on his face.

Chapter Two

Inheritance

My eyes appeared red from crying and felt itchy from lack of sleep. Every time I closed my eyes last night, I heard Grannie's voice. I jerked awake to search the moonlit room, only to find it empty, leaving me bereft and exhausted.

Sitting across from our family retainer, I forced my attention on Wallace Jackson and his words as he prepared to read my grandmother's last will and testament. A tall man with dark hair peppered with gray, he sat forward in his chair with hunched shoulders. Made me wonder if years of sitting in that position had caused the deformity.

Attorney Jackson shuffled a stack of papers on his shiny walnut desk then focused on my dad and me sitting before him.

"Polly had insisted that her will be read immediately following her death. You know how she was; she didn't want any time lost when business needed done. As her legal representative, it's my duty to convey her last wishes regarding the distribution of her estate. So let's get to it." Jackson cleared his throat and nodded to his secretary sitting in the corner, her note pad on her lap. "Let the record show that David James Brooke and Madison Leigh Brooke are both present."

"Will this take long? I've got to get back to take care of the guests at the inn," I crossed my arms over my chest in an attempt to steady my nerves.

"Not long. Shall I begin?"

At my affirmative nod, the lawyer began. His voice sounded measured and solemn as he read, "I, Polly Ann Brooke, being of sound mind, do hereby declare this instrument to be my last will and testament. First, I direct the payment of my lawful debts, funeral expenses, and testamentary charges."

The lawyer paused and looked up from the document then took a deep breath before he continued. "Second, I bequeath all my assets, land, and property, including but not limited to the Magnolia Blossom Inn, to my precious granddaughter, Madison Leigh Brooke, to have and to hold in fee simple absolute, forever. To my son David James Brooke, I leave the sum of twenty-five thousand dollars. Lastly, I appoint Wallace Jackson, Esquire, as executor of my estate, entrusting him with the responsibility of administering my affairs in accordance with the provisions of this will."

"Oh my God! Magnolia Blossom is mine?" I gasped in astonishment.

"Who else would she leave the place to? It's been your home most of your life. I'd expect nothing less from your grandmother," David said.

"You aren't angry that she didn't deed the property to you?" I asked my father as the weight of my inheritance sank in.

"My mother knew I'd never be happy tied to one place. I've got too much wanderlust in my veins. No, sweetie, I'm happy to know you've been provided for and will always have a home."

The attorney interrupted, "Um, well, in conclusion, I hereby affirm the validity of this will and testament, signed and sealed in the presence of witnesses on the twelfth of February, in the year 2020."

Jackson stood and shook hands with my father then came around in front of his desk and enveloped me in a quick embrace. "Naturally, you can count on me to provide you with whatever guidance you need. I'll file all necessary papers to transfer the deed of Magnolia Blossom into your name. David, my office has prepared a check for the specified sum. My secretary will give it to you on your way out."

"Thanks. Mister Jackson, I know you've been friends with my mom for decades. She trusted you. I'm glad Maddie can come to you for advice after I'm back at sea."

I stood up on shaky legs then held out my hand to the lawyer, "Thank you. I'll do everything in my power to honor Grannie's legacy and preserve the Magnolia Blossom Inn as she would have wanted. I just pray I can manage on my own."

"I'm sure you'll do fine. Your grandmother told me how proud she was of you and thought you were a capable young woman."

I followed my father out of the law office then faced him as he stood on the sidewalk gazing at the town square.

"When are you going back? I had hoped we'd have some time together," I asked him.

"Sorry Maddie, but I got a call from the Maersk scheduling office. I leave tonight. They've got a container ship waiting on me in the port of Savannah. I promised I'd be there to take her out on the twenty-third."

I swallowed back unwanted tears and stared at some kids in the park then swung my attention back to the man by my side.

"Where to this time?" I hated hearing the quiver in my voice. Why should I care if he leaves?

"Heading out to Melbourne, Australia. It'll be a long run."

"Yeah, well. You do what you've got to do and I'll do the same. I'll be all right."

We started walking toward our pickup but only got three steps before being stopped by the local town gossip hurrying out of her flower shop.

"Hello Madison. I just wanted to convey my condolences to you and your father. I'm afraid I didn't get a chance to speak with you at the viewing yesterday."

"Thank you Mrs. Ginther. I appreciate your kindness." I tried to step around her, giving her a brief smile and nod, but she moved to block me.

"And will you be staying home now David Brooke? I declare, we haven't seen you around these parts in a coon's age," the old biddy continued in her zest for a juicy tidbit.

"No máam, I'm afraid not. But I'll be back in a few months," my father answered her then clasping my elbow, he steered me into the street and away from the nosy neighbor.

Mrs. Ginther stood with her hands on her hips, shaking her head at our rudeness as we left her standing alone.

Grannie had converted the big 1800 era farmhouse with its three floors into the Magnolia Blossom Inn ten years ago after the death of her beloved husband Charles. It sat on fifty acres of prime land in rural Clarkstown, near the gateway to the Skyline Drive and Shenandoah National Park. The farm included a small orchard of cherry and apple trees. Located within an easy commute to the city of Charlottesville, it was an ideal location for tourists wanting a quiet spot to stay but close enough to nearby historical attractions like Monticello or Michie Tavern.

Growing up there, I loved it. The house and the land inspired me and fueled my imagination. As a child, my playmates were often the colonial figures in my mind. It's probably why I chose to study American history at UVA and major in the American Revolutionary period. Everything about the house, its architecture and history, spoke to me. I found the history of the Jeffersonian region fascinating.

The inn offered five bedrooms with private baths for guests and two bedrooms on the third floor with a shared bath for the owners. The large comfortable living room with a brick hearth opened into a formal dining room boasting an antique mahogany table and Chippendale chairs to accommodate a dozen diners. A polished sideboard buffet standing against one wall held a silver tea service, while a tall grandfather clock chimed in the corner. A pair of swinging doors separated the kitchen and dining room. Down the hall, bookshelves lined the knotty-pine paneling of the small study. A pair of comfortable chairs sat next to a small desk where Grannie liked to do her correspondence and take care of inn business.

Polly Brooke had been born a Stewart. Her Scottish heritage and clan tartan inspired the colors and fabrics of her home. The tartan plaid upholstered the long stuffed sofa; its vibrant red stripes on a white background blended with the plaid overlay of navy blue, yellow, and hunter green stripes. Polly had chosen the solid red color for two wing back side chairs and a coordinating sunny yellow woven fabric for draperies flanked the wide bay window. A third side chair also wore the plaid. A cobalt blue vase filled with wildflowers graced the center of the lace runner atop the dining room table. Framed paintings of the Virginia countryside hung on the walls of both dining and living rooms. The country décor was pleasing to the eye and welcoming to travelers who stayed at the Magnolia Blossom.

Exhibiting southern manners and old-fashioned hospitality, Thomas Borden poured second cups of coffee for the three guests finishing their breakfasts in the inn's dining room. He glanced toward the kitchen door when he heard Maddie and her dad enter.

"Hi folks. Did y'all enjoy your breakfast? I'm sure Tom took excellent care of you," I said, greeting the inn's customers at the dining table.

They murmured their agreements as they finished their breakfast and prepared to head out for a day's adventure.

I smiled at the older couple and their daughter before retreating to the kitchen. We couldn't afford to lose a paying guest and their referrals. It had been a slow spring because of the heavy rains. To compensate, Grannie had offered the inn as a temporary residence for a couple students from UVA. They'd arrive next week. She had been glad to secure the contract with the university while dorms were being remodeled.

As soon as I could find a quiet moment, I planned on going over the accounts and determine just how our bottom line looked. I'd been involved with day-to-day operations of the inn and reception duties for the past five years, but the finance side had been all Grannie's. It was a daunting prospect to realize I was now responsible for all of it. I definitely needed some help. Taking a deep breath and exhaling slowly calmed my frayed nerves and allowed me to stand in the center of the room and absorb the essence of the inn—its living, breathing soul.

Thomas Borden, wearing a long black bib-apron, joined me in the cheerful blue and white kitchen. He began washing pots and pans then finished loading the dishwasher. Thomas wore dual hats of cook and maintenance man around the Magnolia Blossom. I studied Thomas as he worked, knowing Grannie had relied on the competent, unassuming man for years, and I certainly intended to continue his employment. Since the inn served only breakfast to guests, once he finished cooking the meal, his day was free to devote to miscellaneous chores on the property. We served cookies or some type of pastry in the early evening with a beverage or wine with cheese and crackers. Even my meager cooking skills were capable of assembling the evening snack tray.

Moving to the reception desk near the front door, I checked email messages on the computer and listened to the phone's voicemail. Flipping open the appointment book, I penciled in a telephone booking for a three-day stay next week. Studying the calendar, I realized the inn would be vacant for four days after the Wilson family left tomorrow and before the new Jamison booking arrived. Guess I could spend the time doing some spring cleaning and reviewing the accounts. We needed the income, but it might be helpful to have the place to myself for a while.

A mournful whining noise caught my attention, and I went in search of it. Luke pawed at Grannie's bedroom door; his big head turned to me as I neared.

"Hey boy. You miss her too, I know. Come away now, let's go outside," I coaxed the big black and tan German shepherd as I rubbed his head and shoulders.

Luke barked and pawed once again at the closed door. He whimpered and keened his grief for his departed mistress. The sound gave me shivers.

I tried to turn him away, but he steadfastly refused to budge. Maybe he'd settle down if I let him sniff around her room and prove to him it was empty.

"All right; let's have a look." I turned the doorknob and opened the portal into her bedroom with its miniature rose buds covering the walls and its pale mauve carpeting. White lace curtains draped the window. Her collection of cut-glass perfume bottles and miniature vases still adorned the dresser top. I breathed in my grandmother's lingering scent.

Luke instantly pushed his way past me then stopped short in the center of the bedroom.

Following him, I blinked my eyes and stared. It couldn't be. I must be hallucinating.

"Grannie?" I uttered to the ethereal image that hovered within the filtered rays of light shining through the bedroom window.

Luke whimpered and lay on the floor, rolling over in a playful gesture. If it weren't for his actions, I'd swear I had lost my mind. Dunno, maybe I had.

"Maddie, baby girl, don't be afraid," Grannie spoke in a hushed tone. Her voice, so familiar, hung like a whisper on the breeze.

I shook my head and sank to the floor. My legs no longer supported me, as my mind sought to comprehend what my eyes and ears had witnessed.

"How? But ... are you real? Oh, Grannie!"

"Find out what happened to me, Maddie. I won't find peace until I learn who killed me. Protect your inheritance," Grannie's ghost insisted.

Her image faded before my eyes.

"What do you mean? Grannie! Don't go!" I cried.

"I'll be near when you need me," her voice whispered.

Luke barked and jumped to his feet. The room was empty. I sat on the floor next to her bed, clutching its hand-sewn quilt, and trembled. Luke placed a comforting paw on my arm. The room spun dizzily; a groan escaped my mouth before I fainted.

Chapter Three

Ghostly Puzzle

The sound of my name being called from afar broke my stupor. Dragging myself upright, I made my way out of Grannie's bedroom and staggered down the stairs, where I found Lily Chung walking out of the kitchen.

"Hey! I was looking for you. Lionel told me you needed to talk to me," greeted Lily, then stopped and stared at my face. "Holy cow, girl, you look like you've seen a ghost! I swear you're as white as a sheet."

I tried to laugh, but it came out as a hiccup. "I think I just did."

"What? Sit down and let me get you a glass of sweet tea. I've seen bodies in the morgue with more color than you have right now. What's going on?" Lily asked as she rushed back into the kitchen and I heard the refrigerator open then close and glasses rattle in the cabinet. She returned and thrust a glass into my hand.

"Drink."

"Boy you're bossy. Do you treat all your patients like this?" I joked as I sipped the sweet iced-tea and calmed down.

"That's better. Your color is improving. You had me worried there." Lily clasped my hand as she said softly, "I'm so sorry about Grannie. You know I wanted to attend the funeral. I was all set to leave when paramedics brought in victims from a bad traffic accident and the ER got swamped. Just couldn't get away."

"That's okay. I understand. You missed a good luncheon though. Most of Albemarle County turned out, at least the neighbors in this area and close to Charlottesville. Grannie knew a lot of people."

"So what did you want to see me about?" asked Lily as she sipped her own cold tea.

She sat back in her chair and scrutinized me in her all-knowing way, shoving her long black hair off her slim shoulders in a gesture I'd seen her do a thousand times when we were roommates on campus. I used to kid her she must be related to Charlie Chan, possessing the same devious insight and mystique as the famous Asian detective. Although still in an intern status, that trait made Lily a great diagnostician. She was also kind and empathetic and I loved her as sister.

"How much time do you have today? This story may take a while," I said.

Luke trotted across the room, his toenails clicking on the tiled floor before he nosed his way out the light screen door and into the yard. He barked at Prissy, the black and white tuxedo cat who lived in the barn. She, in turn, hissed at him before putting her tail in the air and marched back to her domain and the latest litter of kittens. I smiled as I watched the animals. Life goes on. Now I had to figure out how to do the same.

Carrying our drinks, we retreated outside to the wide wrap- around porch with its comfortable rockers and swings. The porch was a favorite spot for guests to relax, to enjoy the bucolic scenery of the rolling hills and breathe in the fresh country air. The delicate blooms and glossy leaves of the magnolia trees shaded the expansive porch. Baskets of daisies, petunias and primrose hung in intervals along the porch railing. The porch had become a frequent refuge for me, too.

I dropped onto one end of the swing, setting it into motion. Lily sat next to me and waited patiently for me to begin my tale.

"Do you believe in ghosts?" I asked my friend in a hushed voice that made her lean toward me to hear.

"No, but I don't rule out the aura of energy that I've witnessed lingering over a person seconds after they die. I can't explain it but I've felt it. My Chinese ancestors would probably argue that it's the spirit or soul of the person. I'm sure someone of a different religion would have another view. Why? You weren't kidding about seeing a ghost," Lily stated, scrutinizing me.

"You're going to laugh at me, but I spoke to Grannie's ghost today. At least, I think I did. Her image materialized and talked to me. The dog saw her too. Am I losing my mind?"

"Of course not. Grief affects people in many ways. You said she spoke to you. What did she say?" Lily asked, getting right to the point. She steepled her fingers as she listened to me, her attention fully focused. Curiosity gleamed in her eyes.

"Um, she wanted me to find out how she died. She told me she can't be at peace until she knows. That's kind of what I wanted to talk to you about. How can someone be perfectly healthy one day and suddenly die the next? My grandmother seemed to be in excellent health. She stayed busy doing chores around the inn and spoke of her plans for the summer then the next morning I find her dead in the barn."

"Did the medical examiner perform an autopsy?" Lily asked.

"No. Doctor Houser came right away when I called 9-1-1. He didn't call the coroner."

"That old coot. He needs to retire."

"I didn't realize you knew Doctor Houser."

"He taught an anatomy course during my first semester of med school. The old fool stumbled around and mistook a kidney for the pancreas on the 3D model he was using," Lily stated with an unladylike snort.

"Houser insisted it was natural causes ... old age. That's what he listed on the death certificate. I don't believe it, but I didn't push the issue and demand a further examination. Guess I was in too much shock to think logically. Now it's too late."

"It could have been a heart attack, I suppose. What did she have to eat that morning? Could she have had a food allergy? Could she have accidentally eaten poisonous mushrooms or something like that."

Shaking my head no, I stared across the field of gaily colored wildflowers that bordered the fruit orchard and that Grannie had loved so well. I could tell that Lily's analytical mind had categorized possibilities and had begun check lists of known causes.

"I hate to ask this, but did Polly have any enemies? Would someone have wanted to harm her?"

"Everyone loved Grannie. You knew her. There wasn't a dry eye at her funeral. I don't know what to do or think. How am I supposed to get an answer for her? For that matter, how am I going to manage this place all by myself? I don't know if I can." Crossing my arms, I hugged myself and rocked the swing slowly back and forth.

"I don't have an answer for you, Maddie. As a doctor, I recommend you take the next couple of days to mourn and take care of yourself. Don't try to solve all your problems right now. Even the most difficult puzzle can be solved with enough time. Time is what you need now." Lily stole a look at her watch. "Speaking of which, I'm sorry, but I've got to go. You call me if I can help. Okay?"

"Thanks. I will. Maybe we can get together with Lionel and plan a night out. It's been awhile and I could use a break."

"Absolutely. How about a visit to one of the new wine bars downtown near campus? Supposed to be fun," Lily said as she slid behind the wheel of her older, silver Toyota Camry.

"Uh huh. Sounds good. I'll text you."

Chapter Four

Sparkling Spirits

My friends' laughter was music to my ears as I sat back in my chair and relaxed in their warm friendship and the cool breeze of the early evening. I smiled fondly at both Lily and Lionel as I let my mind drift. Tonight I had no worries, no doubts that kept me awake at night. Just close friends and good food to enjoy.

"Lionel, this place is darling. I love the canopy of white lights criss-crossing the patio and all the stone pots filled with daisies. Can't believe we've never been here before. How'd we ever miss it when we were in school?" I asked as I nibbled on a cracker and waited for the waiter to return.

"I know, isn't it? A guy at work told me about it ... said it was a winery I just had to try. So I figured, what could be a better night out?" Lionel smiled his big wide grin at the two of us.

"What's the name of this place again? I might want to recommend it to a couple nurses at the hospital. They love exploring new places on the Monticello Wine Trail." Lily laughed and said, "They think it's doing something historical and excuses getting sloshed on wine."

I picked up a slim brochure and read the information on the owners and the winery description. "Robin Hill Farm and Vineyard, owned by brothers Hank and William Hill. Says here they've been in business for two years. Funny, we never found this place before. Guess our studies and graduation kept us too occupied."

A handsome young waiter returned to our table with an assortment of crackers and cheese cubes. Lionel and he exchanged appraising glances before he shifted his focus on each of us expectantly. "Have you decided what you'd like?"

"Yes. We'd like to have a wine flight with six varieties, please" ordered Lionel.

"Very good sir. May I suggest three white and three red?"

"Great. Bring it on." Lionel watched him slither away suggestively.

The waiter prepared our wine samples and returned with six clean wine glasses for each of us. He poured an ounce of the white zinfandel in each of our glasses for us to taste first.

"I suggest you start with the white, more dry or fruity wines then try the stronger red wine samplings last," the waiter said as he arranged the bottles in order of vintage.

"Mmm, this is good. I like this one. Is that a hint of vanilla? What do you think, Lily?" I asked as I sipped the wine.

"Could be. Your taste buds are more refined than mine. I think it's because disinfectant smells always fill my nostrils—affects your taste if your nose doesn't work."

Lionel snorted at Lily's descriptive excuse. He turned serious as he asked me, "Have you made any decisions, Maddie? Are you going back to finish your master's degree this fall?"

"Honestly, I haven't even considered it. As much as I'd love to bury my head in a pile of musty history books and pretend I lived during colonial days, I just can't. Without Grannie, Magnolia Blossom is my responsibility now. I've been spending the last couple of days going through the accounts and trying to figure out where I can cut expenses to get us through the season. I have a new family booked for next week and then a couple of students will be arriving at the inn for the two month summer break. Their dorm is under renovation and

Grannie had negotiated a contract with the university housing department to be a student residence. That's a guaranteed income which helps."

"I didn't realize the inn was in trouble," Lily commented.

"It's not, really. Just that we have operating expenses, property taxes due, and this spring was so wet with weeks of rain that, of course, tourists stayed away. We counted on bookings during Easter and now I'm feeling the pinch. But I'll manage. We've got the cherry festival coming up soon and that always generates income. As Grannie used to say, 'it'll all come out in the wash.'"

"Maybe you need a marketing campaign. Do you have an updated web site? I could help with that," Lionel suggested.

"We have a basic web site. It probably doesn't get many hits. I'd love for you to do your magic and create an exciting page that could attract more business. Would y'all really do that for me? I'd pay you, of course. I don't expect you to spend your time without compensation."

"If you don't mind my working on it at night, we can whip up a commanding page. Don't worry about my fee, that's what friends are for." Lionel grinned at me and I knew my worries were for naught.

Focusing on sipping the rosé and tasting its fruity flavor, I allowed myself to scan the crowd filling the outdoor patio seating and brazenly people watched. As my finger toyed with a lock of my blond hair, my eyes settled on a particularly handsome guy with wavy dark hair and a closely trimmed dark beard and mustache. He stood among a small circle of people listening to one man talk. His lethal looks aroused me, even from a distance. When he turned his head, I noticed the fringe of his hair curled just above the collar of his shirt. My fingers ached to run through the thick mass; I sighed and squelched my shocking desire.

Lily turned in her chair to look behind her. "Who did you see? Your mouth just dropped open."

"Hmm? Oh, no one. That is ... do you know that guy over there? The one with the dark hair and he's wearing a white shirt and pair of chinos." I hesitated to point in the direction of my desire.

Lionel and Lily both followed my direction. Lily shook her head no, but Lionel grinned.

"Mmm, I'd say I saw him first, but I can see the lust in your eyes, Maddie girl. The gentleman is one of Charlotteville's new detectives. You've got great taste; I admired him myself the first time he stopped by the office."

My cheeks felt hot as a blush colored my skin. My gosh, was I so easy to read? When did I openly ogle a man in public? Grannie would surely chastise me for being wanton.

"What's his name? You said he came by your office. Was there a problem at the center?" I asked.

Lionel headed the information technology security office of the African-American Heritage Center in Charlottesville. In school, he had concentrated on computer forensics and security, and naturally, upon graduation, his services were in high demand. Although he'd had several offers from big name corporations, Lionel had chosen to stay local and devote his energies to the center that meant so much to him.

"We had one of our affiliates experience a computer hack. I reported it to the police because of the security breach to their confidential financial data. Detective Allen Crawford responded. Seems like a nice guy."

"Hmm, you said he's a new detective. Does that mean he's not from around here or just recently promoted?"

"Actually both. He has a wicked accent, bit harsh on the ears, from Philadelphia. The man is a Yankee transplanted to our fair land of magnolias." Lionel sipped a glass of merlot and reached for a buttery town house cracker.

"Well bless his heart," remarked Lily.

Laughing, I almost spilled my wine. "Lily I think you've lived too long in Virginia; y'all starting to sound like one of us."

I couldn't help staring at the topic of our conversation and mentally filed away the name and information that Lionel had shared. *Maybe our paths would cross one day. Wouldn't that be nice?*

My cell phone buzzed in my purse and I rushed to grab it before the caller hung up. I glanced at the caller I.D. as I answered the call. Setting down my cup of coffee, I took a deep breath before answering.

"Hello Bobbie Jo. How are you?"

"Hey Maddie. How y'all holding up? I've been thinking of you but didn't want to phone too soon."

Bobbie Jo Taylor claimed second, or maybe it was third, cousin relationship to me on my mother's side of the family. The only girl among three brothers, and the youngest child in the family ... to say she was spoiled would be an understatement. Two years younger than me, she studied art history at UVA and was finishing her junior year. Her petulant voice came across the cell phone as she rambled on about her latest class. I half listened to her speech, recalling the many times as kids that she managed to get both of us into trouble. Somehow, I was the only one who took the blame and the punishment.

"I don't recall seeing you at the funeral," I broke into her monologue.

"Um, sorry, I went out of town last week. A group of us from class traveled to New York to visit the Metropolitan Museum of Art. I'd already paid for the plane ticket and admission to the museum and just couldn't cancel. Y'all understand, don't you?" Bobbie Jo's voice pleaded.

"Of course. No worries. So what's up?"

"Well ... I was wondering if I could stay at the inn during summer break? I was thinking of painting a series of scenes around the farm and house as my senior thesis. You know, colonial property ... the history of the land and all that. Really, Magnolia Blossom would be the perfect subject. So, can I?"

Taking a deep breath and leave of my common sense, I gave in to her request. "If I say yes, can you help out around the inn? Give me a hand running the office, housekeeping, or catering to guests? I could use the extra pair of hands and you'd be earning your keep; I wouldn't charge you any room and board."

Bobbie Jo squealed in delight, forcing me to hold the phone away from my ear.

"Is that a yes? I mean it, Bobbie Jo, you'll have to work."

"Yes! I promise to be as useful as I can. You just tell me what to do and I'll do it," she promised. "Can I move in on May first?"

"Bobbie Jo, that's only four days away. I thought the semester didn't end until the tenth of May?"

"I know, but that's just a technicality. The senior art majors are beginning work on our projects, therefore, I don't have to stay on campus. So, can I?"

"Of course. I'll get your room ready. Maybe I'll move into Grannie's old room and you can take mine. Four days should give me enough time to get stuff packed and moved."

"Super! See you then," Bobbie Jo enthused then ended the call.

"I hope I'm making the right decision," I told Luke as he propped his snout on my lap and I absentmindedly scratched his head. "C'mon boy, let's go upstairs and see what needs to be done."

Luke barked as I opened the bedroom door. My ears detected a hauntingly familiar tune. Grannie's ghost sat on the side of the bed, humming softly, as if she was expecting me. She smiled at Luke as he barked again and spun in circles around her feet.

Chapter Five

Hidden Memories

"*Whew! You have no idea the amount of energy it takes for me to appear, but I think I'm finally getting the hang of this,*" Grannie said in a whispery voice that hung in the air.

"Oh my gosh, you really are here. I had convinced myself that I had dreamt you, or simply imagined you after the funeral. I need to sit down," I croaked.

My voice caught in my throat as I neared her transparent image. Reaching out to embrace Grannie, my hand passed through her body and only touched the bedding. Shuddering, I jerked back and raised my eyes to her in wonder.

"*Sorry, baby girl, I want to hold you too, but I can't. Being a ghost has its limits.*" She laughed. Her melodious chuckle floated around me.

Smiling, I recalled the many times I had heard that beautiful sound while sitting on the porch or picking apples in the orchard. Grannie loved telling a good story, especially a funny tale, and wasn't embarrassed to share her humor. In the past, her laughter pealed throughout the house.

"Uh, are you stuck in this room? I mean ... can you move about the house?" I asked as my eyes became accustomed to seeing her like this.

"I'm pretty sure I can move about the house. Honestly, I haven't tried yet. I was in the hallway the other day when those folks left ... the husband walked right through me. Kind of tickled."

"What?! You were in the hall when the Wilson family left? Did they see you?"

"No, certainly not. You're the only person who can see me, and Luke of course. Animals have a sixth sense about them; Luke will always be able to see or smell my presence."

The big German shepherd raised his head and pawed at the side of the bed as if he knew he was part of the conversation.

"Why can I see you and no one else can?" I asked.

"I suppose because you loved me more than anyone else. We shared a bond so close that even death couldn't break it. Have you learned anything about how I died?" Grannie asked.

"No, not yet. I promise I'll try." Summoning my courage, I asked her, "Will it be okay if I move into your bedroom? I feel odd about removing your things. Bobbie Jo called. She wants to live here for a couple months this summer so I told her she could have my room and I thought I'd take this one. Is that going to be awkward?" I paced back and forth by the foot of the bed, glanced out the window then back at Grannie.

"Bobbie Jo is coming to live here? I thought you had had enough of that chit. Whatever possessed you?"

"I was thinking of the inn. I'm worried. We could use some more help around here and I wouldn't have to pay her a salary."

"You expect Bobbie Jo to do some work? This should prove entertaining. I'm looking forward to seeing that." Grannie's laugh floated across the room.

"I'm already regretting my decision. This room may become my refuge. Are you sure it's okay if I move into your bedroom?"

"The place is yours now. Naturally, you should occupy the master bedroom." Grannie blew me a kiss as she began to fade and just like that, she was gone.

Staring at the empty space, I shook my head to clear it. I'd have to get used to Grannie's sudden coming and going, especially if I ever hoped to find sleep in her room.

Sunset cast an orange glow onto the floor as I raised the window. A warm breeze caressed my skin as I leaned on the sill; the lace curtains fluttered like a bride's trailing veil. An overwhelming sense of peace suddenly washed over me.

The house sat quiet with no guests. Tom had left for the day and returned to his solitary home up the road; he'd be back at six in the morning to start his normal routine. That left just Luke and me. Luke stretched out in the middle of the bedroom floor with his head resting on his front legs, watching me drag the empty suitcase from the closet and onto the bed. Ever since Grannie's death, I noticed the dog stayed by my side or preferred to be in the same room with me. Protecting me. His presence comforted me.

Pulling open dresser drawers, I emptied my grandmother's clothing —her nightgowns, underclothes, and camisoles. I sorted through the items, setting aside the camisoles that I could wear and one of her favorite nighties that I couldn't bear to part with. The rest I packed into the suitcase. Figured using a suitcase would help me carry the clothing to the Goodwill store, and since I couldn't find any large cardboard boxes, this would have to do.

Next came the closet. I stood before the open door and looked at the garments hanging there. Grannie really didn't have that many clothes. Like many women of her generation, her Sunday best outfits hung on one side of the closet, with her more practical dresses and blouses grouped together on the other side. Removing one flowery print dress with a lace collar, I sniffed Grannie's favorite perfume that still clung to the fabric. Reverently, I folded the garment and placed it into the suitcase, brushing a tear from my eye. This was going to be harder than I thought.

My fingers caressed the soft wool of Grannie's favorite shawl draped over a hangar. I left it in the closet, not wanting to part with it. Wearing it, I'd feel wrapped within Grannie's warm embrace. That thought made me smile.

Folding the handful of remaining dresses and blouses, I added them to the suitcase and closed the lid. The closet stood empty save for two pairs of shoes and a pair of worn slippers on the floor. A hat box sat in the corner of the top shelf. I had to reach on tippy-toes to snag the edge of the box with my fingertips then slide it toward the front. Finally ... I lifted the hat box and carried it to the dresser top.

A faded pink satin ribbon encircled the box, holding the lid in place, and tied in a bow. Pulling the ends of the bow loose, I slid the ribbon off and removed the lid. Tissue paper filled the round box and nestled in the middle was a white pill-box hat with an attached veil. An alluring, time-less hat, reminiscent of the iconic style worn by former First Lady Jackie Kennedy in the 1960s.

I looked at it in wonder then gingerly picked up the silk hat to study it closer. The hat's veil netting clung to the tissue paper, pulling it upward and revealed a stack of tied notes beneath. Could they be love letters Grannie had saved and hidden away? Who wrote them? The thought piqued my curiosity but also stirred feelings of guilt, snooping into the private life of my grandmother. I wondered if the age of the hat had anything to do with the date of the love letters. I'd never know unless I read one. The historian in me itched to explore the vintage papers. Did I dare, or should I wait to question Grannie's ghost?

Chapter Six

Grannie's Secret

I needed a glass of wine for courage before digging into my grandmother's past. Carrying the packet of letters, I headed to the kitchen with Luke trotting along at my heels. The historic hardwood floors squeaked familiarly as I walked downstairs and through the vacant house. A low lamp burned in the living room bay window and Tom had left a light turned on over the kitchen sink. I knew it was a waste of electricity, but those two orbs of illumination made me feel safer and not so alone in the big house.

Sipping a glass of white zin from the bottle I'd bought at the Robin Hill Winery, I untied the bundle of parchment letters and removed the first one. My eyes skimmed the slanted handwriting and my eyebrows raised as I read the tender confession of love. Sighing, I thought back to my high school boyfriend that I had been terribly in love with at the time, or so I'd thought. I definitely never received any passionate letters from him; heck, he never even sent me a Valentine's card without his mother reminding him. Oh, to be loved so deeply by a man for him to pour out his heart in such beautiful words. I closed my eyes, twirled a lock of hair around my finger and savored the moment before continuing to read more.

Suddenly, a gust of cold air filled the room, sweeping the fragile paper off the table. When I bent to retrieve the note from the floor, Grannie's solid body stood before me. The letter in question levitated in the air. To say it was unsettling would be an understatement.

"How dare you pry into my most private belongings? Those letters were written to me, not meant for you to read. Put them away, right now! You aren't going to find an answer to my death in there."

"I'm sorry, Grannie. I found them in your hat box." I carefully gathered up the bundle of letters and tied them again with the faded ribbon. "I only read a little in one note; his words were beautiful. Did Grandpop Charlie send you these?"

Her spectral image wore an angry countenance as she flitted about the room as if she were pacing the floor. I waited for her to speak, trying to recall when my grandmother ever exhibited such a fiery temper. Somehow I doubted the author of those passionate missives was my grandfather or she wouldn't be acting like this.

"What would you like me to do with these, Grannie? I guess I can stuff them back into that hat box and leave it on the closet shelf, but Bobbie Jo might find them. Do you want me to burn them?" I asked her spirit as she came to rest before me.

"Yes, burn them. I should never have kept them. Someone I once considered marrying wrote those letters when I was a young girl. That's all I'll say on the matter. Get rid of them," she insisted.

As I stood up and reached for the bundle of letters, a puff of cold air ruffled my hair and she was gone. Wow, Grannie was getting better at making a grand entrance and exit.

Determined to abide by her wishes, I walked into the living room and threw some kindling onto the fireplace logs. Lighting the scraps of wood, I cautiously added the paper bundle until it took hold and the flames whisked away the words of devotion from years ago. Gosh, I wish I'd had the chance to at least read the signature. I wondered who the man in my Grannie's life had been or, for that matter, where was he now?

I rose early after a troubled sleep; feelings of regret and guilt over my actions of the night before kept filling my mind. I felt like I had abused Grannie's trust by invading her privacy with those love letters. Dressing in a pair of jeans and a tee shirt, I entered the kitchen and started the morning pot of coffee just as Tom entered the back door.

"You're up early. Something wrong?" he asked me, a frown wrinkled his brow.

"No, nothing's wrong. Just have a lot to do today and wanted to make an early start. Don't bother cooking anything this morning. I'm gonna have a bowl of cereal and some fruit. I could use your help today though, moving a bookcase from my room into Grannie's bedroom if you have some time. I'll be moving into the front room. My cousin Bobbie Jo will stay with us this summer to help out; she'll occupy my old room."

Tom nodded and raised an eyebrow at my statement but didn't make any comment. "Sure, just holler when you're ready and I'll give you a hand."

Breakfast finished, I washed up the few dishes and headed upstairs with one small box that I'd found in the garage. I started by packing Grannie's collection of cut-glass perfume bottles and miniature vases into the carton. I'll have to find a special place for them somewhere in the house. After clearing the dresser space and top of the chest, I gathered up my own belongings and carried them into my new bedroom. I placed the mirrored tray holding my favorite perfume, three bottles of nail polish, hair brush and comb, and a tube of hand cream onto the center of the dresser. I added one of Grannie's small vases next to the tray. Maybe later I could pick some flowers to put in it.

I stood before the dresser and raised my eyes to stare at the face in the mirror. A doubtful young woman with blond hair in need of a trim, intelligent blue eyes that had turned wary, looked back at me. Someone forced to contemplate being solely responsible for maintaining a large property and business. The enormity of it all scared me to death. What will become of Magnolia Blossom if I fail? I shook my head and straightened my shoulders; I couldn't let my thoughts dwell there. Back to the task at hand.

Tossing a bundle of clothes over my arm, I made quick work of hanging my things in the empty closet. It wasn't hard to see that I owned a lot more clothes than Grannie had, mine quickly filled the closet. I suppose my generation wasn't as thrifty as our elder's or it might mean we put more emphasis on material things. An idea to ponder later.

I decided to strip both beds and wash up all the linens fresh for both Bobbie Jo and me. The quilts and bedspreads would stay in each room after airing them on the clothesline in the bright sunshine. By the time I had loaded the laundry, the only thing left to do was move the bookcase between the rooms. Emptying the four shelves, I stacked my books onto the floor where I'd retrieve them later.

"Ready for me now?" asked Tom as he rounded the corner and peeked into my bedroom. The man had an uncanny sixth sense when it came to knowing he was needed.

"Think so. I scooted over the chest of drawers and made room for the bookcase in the corner, so we just need to carry it in. It's more awkward than heavy and I was afraid I'd ding the door frame if I moved it myself."

"Sure, no problem."

Five minutes later, the bookcase nestled in the corner and Tom brought in a stack of my books to fill the shelves. Looking at the assortment of history tomes and biographies, I smiled as the room became more my own.

"Hey, Tom, you've been here a long time. Haven't you?"

"Yeah, guess you could say that. Reckon I started working for your grandpa in the orchard before he died, so that makes it about eighteen years. Why?"

"Did Grannie ever talk about anyone from her past? I mean, did you ever see anybody ... a man visiting, maybe an old beau? You know what I mean." I exhaled in embarrassment.

"No máam. I can't say that I did, and I don't think your Grannie would appreciate you speculating or starting gossip out of turn," Tom scolded me with a severe look.

I heard his footsteps plodding down the stairs. He left me standing in the middle of the room, ashamed of my brazen questions. How was I going to learn who the mysterious author was of Grannie's love letters? I remembered she said it was someone she once considered marrying, so it had to have been before Grandpa Charles. Tom was right about one thing though, Grannie would not appreciate my investigating her youthful love life. I quickly glanced over my shoulder, expecting her ghostly figure to pop in.

She had asked me to protect Magnolia Blossom and to search for her killer. That task felt so daunting. Taking a deep breath, I decided to consider this like any historical research project and begin at the beginning. Research is what I did best. History was history, and personal records even more so. I'd start with digging into whatever boxes of records existed here at the farm plus explore the official documents on file with the county.

I needed to learn as much as possible about the history of the property and the people in Grannie's past. Who would want her dead and why? I couldn't stop myself from thinking of the mysterious author of those burnt letters, too.

Chapter Seven

Suspicions

With a straw basket slung over my arm and an apron tied about my waist, I left the house the next morning in search of eggs. Daily chores couldn't be forgotten just because I had a research project in mind. First things first, as Grannie always said.

Grandpa Charles had built a sturdy, elevated chicken coop attached to the southeastern side of the barn. Four hens and a rooster shared the roomy twenty-square foot roost with a fenced yard and run that allowed them plenty of room to peck around in the warm sunshine safe from predators. Even Prissy respected the hens and left them alone.

I tossed a handful of chicken feed into the yard and the girls all ran toward it. While they ate, I took advantage of their absence to unlatch the door and enter the coop. My hand searched among the nesting boxes and retrieved a dozen eggs. I placed the eggs gently in my basket and retreated, latching the door securely behind me.

Every time I collected eggs, the memory of being attacked and pecked by a hen as I poked my hand into her nest came rushing back to me, making me shudder. Gosh, I was probably about ten years old and Grannie had tasked me with getting the day's eggs. What an experience! That old hen squawked and defended her nest and sent me rushing out of the coop. The door flew open and eggs splattered on the floor where I had dropped my basket. Hens followed me, running out the open door, causing Grannie and Tom to drop what they were doing to round them back up. Pure chaos. I don't know who cried the louder ... me or the hens. Then the next day, Grannie made me return to the henhouse to collect the eggs and face my fears. I shook my head in memory. That old hen eventually wound up gracing our dinner table. Likely, her great-grandchildren are the chicks strutting around in the pen today.

Welcoming the warm sunshine on my face, I turned my head and spotted Luke chasing a butterfly among the flowers in the orchard. The big shepherd romped in the warm air and relished stretching his legs. A sound in the barn drew my attention. Prissy lay on her side with three wiggling kittens nursing contentedly. I walked into the cool shadows to investigate further, wondering why Luke hadn't barked an alarm. I was surprised to find Attorney Jackson standing near one stall. He turned to face me as I entered.

"Oh, uh, Maddie. There you are. I was looking for you and thought I heard you in here."

"What can I do for you, Mr. Jackson?" It seemed odd to find him there. Why didn't he go up to the house when he arrived, and for that matter, where was his car? I glanced back out in the yard; only our old Dodge Ram pickup truck was parked in the lot.

The lawyer moved away from the empty stall where once Grandpa had stored two old Army footlockers. Grannie had emptied those steel containers just last year and donated the lockers to the local American Legion post. I don't recall what they had held.

"Actually, Maddie, I've got some papers for you to sign regarding the property," Jackson stated.

For the first time, I noticed the briefcase in his hand. "C'mon up to the house. I'll fix you a cup of coffee or if you'd like, perhaps something cold to drink?"

"Coffee is okay."

I led the way across the graveled yard to the back door of the house and we entered the kitchen.

"I didn't see your car. Don't tell me you walked here."

"No, no. I'm too old to be hoofing it. I parked near the entrance to your drive on the paved surface. Um, I just washed my car and didn't want the gravel dust to get all over it if I drove up closer."

He appeared embarrassed with his excuse, whether he thought it might insult me or imply that his car was more important ... I don't know. I let it slide, but he acted awfully nervous.

Setting the basket on the countertop, I washed my hands at the sink then poured us both a cup of coffee. With a wave of my hand, I indicated for him to take a seat at the kitchen table.

"Milk? Sugar?" I asked, placing the cup before him.

"No thanks. Black is fine." Jackson unbuckled the strap on his case and withdrew a sheaf of papers. He handed me one of those lengthy legal documents and pointed to the yellow tab stuck on the bottom line where I needed to sign.

Reading the legal property description and plat location on the deed, I skimmed the rest of the document then accepted the pen offered by the attorney, ready to sign. Until ...

I almost missed the notation of a lien filed against the land. Studying the recent date and dollar amount noted, I blinked in disbelief. I searched for the plaintiff's name on the nonconsensual judgment lien. What was that all about? Why didn't Attorney Jackson say anything about a fifty-thousand dollar judgment being due? Oh my God, how will I pay that kind of money?

"What's this?" My voice rose to a shriek.

"This is the deed. You just need to sign below your name exactly as it's typed." His calm demeanor acted like there was nothing amiss.

"I know it's the deed. What I'm questioning is this lien. Did it slip your mind that an outstanding bill is due on the property? I thought all Grannie's debts were to be paid upon her death and administration of the will?"

"Hmm, let me see. You shouldn't have any problem paying that debt. You can always sell. I could get you a fair price for this property. I'm aware of several developers interested in the land that had previously approached your grandmother. Buyers are out there, just say the word." He took another swallow of his coffee.

"Did my grandmother know about this debt? I can't believe she would abide by a lien on her home. What was it for and who is this person named on the lien?"

"I really can't say if she knew or not. Judgment liens are often filed without the debtors' awareness. Now, if you want to accept your inheritance as directed by the will, you need to sign here," Jackson stated as he pointed to the document. "Of course, as your lawyer, I have to advise you that by doing so you are acknowledging the debt and accepting responsibility for it."

He watched me sign my full name. "That's right and initial here and here." He pointed to two other paragraphs. "Okay. This is your copy and I'll retain one with my records. Of course, the original is recorded at the Albemarle County courthouse."

Grinding my teeth, I spit out, "Thank you." Inwardly seething, I tried to maintain a calm exterior and mind my manners like Grannie taught me, but it was difficult.

"How's it going around here? I noticed you don't seem to have any guests." I watched him glance around, coveting all that he took in, almost chortling to himself.

"No, not this week but I'm expecting a family to check in on Sunday and my cousin will move in for the summer too. The cherry festival starts soon and the place will be swarming with folks."

"Well, as I said, if you, uh, ever decide to sell ..."

"Thanks, but I don't have any plans to sell our family land and give up my inheritance. I'll earn that money some other way." I said defiantly. Standing on the porch, I watched him walk the five hundred or so feet back to his car. *What a creep!*

I returned to the kitchen to clear away our coffee cups and found the deed suspended above the table top as Grannie read the document.

"That scalawag! The nerve of that man trying to get you to sell out. Don't let him steal our land. You've got to protect it. Always suspected he might be a crook and now I know it for sure," Grannie proclaimed in a strong voice.

"Did you know about a fifty-thousand dollar debt filed against the property?"

"No, of course not. What are you talking about? Charles and I always paid our bills; we didn't have any debt. This land was free and clear, only annual taxes due," Grannie insisted.

"Well, according to this paperwork, there's a lien filed on the land. I'm gonna fight this. Now I wonder what he was really doing here? I caught him in the barn looking around. He didn't need to bring by those papers; I could have gone to his office. I thought you trusted the man and he'd been your lawyer for years." I waited to hear Grannie's reply.

"He represented Charlie and me when we got married and we took over the family homestead in 1964. Charlie wanted it all legal like and insisted the deed be registered in our names after his folks died. Never had any reason to doubt Jackson before this but he's been acting strange for months. He pestered me to sell our property, as if he'd benefit somehow. You stand your ground; don't let him convince you to give up this place."

"I won't. I swear I'll protect Magnolia Blossom, but I don't know how I'm ever going to raise that kind of money before the note is called in. What are we going to do?"

"I have faith in you, baby girl, you'll figure a way."

"Grannie, can you remember anything about the morning you died? When you went out to the barn, what were you doing? Was there anyone there? Can you give me some information to go on? I know I promised you to learn what happened but I need your help too," I said.

"All I remember was hearing Luke barking and carrying on so I

walked over to the barn from the chicken coop. I had planned on collecting the eggs like I did every morning but I got side-tracked by Luke's fussing."

"What happened next? You walked into the barn. Was Luke inside?"

"No, I didn't see Luke but I could hear him growling. That's all I know. Next thing I felt was a hand over my mouth and one on my throat, then I fell onto the ground. I guess that's when you found me," Grannie said in a whisper. Her image faded; I was left staring at the empty space as I pondered her words.

Facts. I needed facts to get a clear picture of this land and its history. Could there be more claims on the deed or co-owners? Was that why Grannie was killed? What was Jackson up to? Did those developers resort to murder to steal the land? Who could have been hiding in the barn, waiting for her? If only Luke could speak. I wish I had an answer to my questions. My mind spun with possibilities.

Running upstairs to my room, I slipped on a clean sleeveless blouse over my jeans and brushed my hair into a high ponytail. I gathered up a notebook and pen, along with my purse and keys. Folding the legal papers, I stuffed them into my bag. I passed Tom in the yard as he came out of the barn toward the car park.

"Hey, Tom. I'm headed into town. I might swing by campus too and won't be back for awhile. You okay here alone? "

"Sure. Can I do anything to help?"

"No. Just need to do some research in the library and courthouse. See you later," I told him.

As soon as I walked toward the truck, Luke ran to my side, ready to jump in. Bending down, I scratched his massive head and rubbed his ears.

"Not today boy. You need to stay home."

I climbed into the pickup and headed out toward Charlottesville.

Chapter Eight

Family History

Heading out on state route 250, I had forgotten how congested the traffic could be. It took twenty-five minutes to drive the fifteen miles between Clarkstown and Charlottesville, making me check the time on my watch and worry about whether the courthouse closed during lunch break. I found a parking space along Jefferson Street close to the courthouse. Running up the tall flight of steps, I passed through its classical columns and portico to the front entrance. Once inside the huge marble foyer, I moved to the directory plaque and scanned the office names and floor locations. With my destination in mind, I hopped into the elevator and rode up to the third floor.

The county clerk's office recorded all land transfers and maintained Grantor and Grantee books of deeds. I greeted the clerk as I entered the office.

"Hello. I'd like to do some research on my family's property. May I browse through your books?"

"Do y'all have the legal description of the property and names on the deed?"

At my positive nod, she continued, "You'll find the Grantor books on the left side and Grantee records on the right shelves. You're welcome to use one of the conference tables behind the stacks. Please return each book to its bookcase when you're done." The clerk smiled politely at me then lowered her eyes and returned to her work.

"Thank you kindly," I said as I moved between the tall shelves and read the names and dates on the thick book spines.

Grannie had told me the deed was registered in Grandpa Charles' name in 1964, so that's where I decided to start. Running my finger along the spines as I searched for the correct date range, I stopped when I located the 1960s decade.

Pulling the heavy volume from its shelf, I carried it to one of the empty tables and started carefully turning pages, trying not to crease the corners of the fragile paper. Finally, on page ninety-one, I found the deed showing Charles and Polly Brooke as the Grantees, receiving the inherited property from Charles A. Brooke, Senior and Mary Brooke. A cross-reference linked Charles Senior's name to the Grantors Albert Brooke and Sara Leander Brooke in 1935. I didn't find any other claims to the land that would justify that current judgment lien. I had to keep searching.

I quickly scribbled dates and names in my notebook and went to seek the older book. Wow, with all these deed transfers, it was like looking at my family tree. According to these records, the Brooke family kept the land, passing it down to each male heir until now. Skipping a generation with my father, my inheritance marked the first female of the family to receive the property. Suddenly, I felt the weight of ownership of this historic land settle upon my shoulders.

I returned the heavy tome to its bookcase and pulled out the 1930s volume. Turning the yellowed pages, I finally found the record of Albert and Sara Brooke listed as Grantors in 1935, confirming my reference for the property being transferred to Charles Brooke, Senior. Now I needed to find when Albert first gained the estate. At the bottom of the page, I read a notation of the original owners' name of Thomas Brooke and Camilla Lord Brooke in 1890. Beside that entry, a second note described a separate parcel of land comprising fifty acres deeded to Earl Jackson during 1935. *Hmm, that's interesting.*

The estate must have contained twice as much land before 1935. Did the family sell the land to Jackson or lose it to him? It wasn't unusual for parcels of land to be gambled in high stake poker games or horse races, especially in the South. Many a landowner gained or lost property that way. I wondered if Earl Jackson was a past relative to our lawyer, Wallace Jackson.

Studying the long line of descendants in my notebook, I scribbled a capital "G" next to Grannie and Grandpa Charles' name for grandparent. Then I marked GG for great-grandparent and so on, going down the list to keep track of all the generations. Next, I went to retrieve the Grantee book from 1890 to learn more.

The faded ink caused difficulty in reading the ancient handwriting on the pages. I snapped a picture of it with my phone then enlarged the image to help me decipher the legal description of the real estate. It clearly listed one hundred acres total. Proof the Brooke estate definitely contained a larger parcel of land before 1935. Thinking back to my knowledge of American history, I speculated on whether the family sold land because of the Great Depression. Perhaps the family needed money and sold half of the estate in order to survive. My mind whirled with possible reasons for the transfer. I must remember to ask Grannie if she knew of the earlier acreage disposal.

Reading the names on the deed, I found Thomas Brooke and his wife Camilla Lord and saw where Thomas had inherited the land in 1865 from his father, Aaron Brooke, and wife Martha Jackson Brooke. The Lord name struck a bell, but I couldn't recall where I'd seen it before. Studying the document, I saw that Aaron and Martha were the original owners of the land purchased in 1830.

My eyes widened as I realized there was that Jackson name again. It seemed our families intertwined over the generations. Wouldn't it be interesting if Wallace Jackson turned out to be the mysterious lover who Grannie almost married? Would that be possible? Were our families related on the ancestral tree? Was he the type of man who Grannie could have loved? His current actions seemed to deny that hypothesis.

I closed the heavy book. A puff of dust rose from the worn leather binding, causing me to cough. I slid it back onto its shelf and picked up my notebook and pen. My research completed, I decided to visit the police station for one more nagging question that needed answering.

Stopping at the front desk, I told the clerk, "I put back all the books. I'm leaving now." The clock on the wall showed almost two hours had past.

"Thank you. Y'all have a nice day." The clerk said with a nod and continued typing on the keyboard.

I walked the two-block distance between the courthouse and the police station. Entering the main door, I approached the officer at the front desk. Now that I was here, I really didn't know where to begin.

"Can I help you, miss?" the desk sergeant asked.

Gripping my purse, I shuffled my feet, and tried to form a lucid question in my mind. "Um ... I guess I ..."

My stammer was interrupted by a plain clothes detective entering the vestibule. I raised my eyes to recognize the object of my people watching from the winery. He was even more handsome up close. *How was a girl supposed to think in his presence?* I quickly glanced away.

"Hello," Detective Allen Crawford greeted as he approached me. I remained standing like a forlorn child in a crowd. "You look a bit lost." He stared at me, waiting for an answer.

"Yes suh, guess I am." My voice slipped into a heavy southern accent when I felt super nervous ... like now. I mentally cringed, knowing how I must sound to this Yankee.

"How about you follow me and you can explain what brings you here. I'm Detective Crawford." He opened the connecting doors and politely waved me through with a nod toward the grinning sergeant.

We proceeded down a short hallway and entered one of those office cubicles with four-foot walls topped with plexiglass partitions. The detective sat behind his desk and I took one of the straight back chairs next to it. He leaned forward, elbows on the desk blotter, and patiently waited for me to begin.

"Um, now that I'm here, I really don't know how to explain what I need." *Why did I feel like a wilting flower in front of this man? I couldn't concentrate staring at this gorgeous hunk.*

"That's okay, just start at the beginning. Take your time."

"Well, basically, it's about my grandmother's death." My voice dwindled to barely a whisper. I dropped my handbag onto the floor and clasped my hands in my lap as I tried to calm my nerves.

"Your grandmother's death ... when did she die? Are you reporting her death today? Has there been an accident or homicide?" The officer hastened to grab a notepad and pen. His attitude switched from solicitous to suspicious, and I heard his distinct Yankee accent.

"Oh, no, Grannie died ten days ago. We had her funeral and everything ... that's the problem. I mean ... goodness gracious, how do I ask this without sounding ridiculous?" I wrung my hands, swallowed, then blurted, "the death certificate stated natural causes but I don't believe that and I want to find out what happened, what killed her. How do I do that?"

"I see. Let's start with the basics. What is your name and what is the name of the deceased? You said she died ten days ago. Was there an autopsy?" In a level voice; he questioned me in a clipped, professional tone.

I took a deep breath and exhaled before answering. "My name is Madison Brooke and my grandmother was Polly Brooke. She died on April 18th at home. No, there wasn't any autopsy and now I suppose it's too late."

"Why do you think there's some cause for her death other than natural? Do you have a reason to be suspicious?"

How could I explain to the detective that Grannie's ghost told me she died of foul play?

"It's just that ... Grannie was always as healthy as a horse and was perfectly fine the morning that she died. She went out to the barn and then I found her lying on the ground dead. Doesn't that seem strange to y'all?"

"Well, I'm sure it must have been a shock for you, but I'm sorry, people do drop dead from heart attacks or stroke all the time. How old was your grandmother? Was her doctor present?"

"Grannie was seventy-nine. Yes, Doctor Houser came right out when I called; he was there in minutes. He's the one that said it was just old age, but I simply can't accept that. I feel like I need to do something, but I don't know what. Can y'all help me?"

"The only way to know for certain is to exhume the body and perform an autopsy. I'd need some type of evidence before requesting the court's permission to perform that," Detective Crawford explained as he studied me.

"Oh my gracious! Disturb Grannie's grave?" I asked in a voice that sounded straight out of *Gone With The Wind* as I contemplated the horrible thought.

Was I prepared to take such a drastic step?

Chapter Nine

Ashes to Clues

"Here's my card. Call me if you have any more questions," Crawford said. The tone of his voice implied the opposite of his words. He rose in a gesture of dismissal. "I'm here most of the time."

"Surely you spend time with your family, detective? I hope y'all don't live at the police station." I flashed him a sweet smile to accompany that leading question dripping honeysuckle, doing justice to any southern belle. As soon as the words were out of my mouth, I regretted my bold question. *What was I thinking?!*

He coughed, his face reddened slightly under the beard, then replied, "I don't have a family, er, that is ... I'm single. Just moved here, so I hang out at the station."

I accepted the plain black and white business card, noting his cell phone number listed a Philadelphia area code. Tucking it into my purse, my fingers brushed the edge of the Magnolia Blossom's cards in a pocket of my bag and I pulled one out.

"Since we're exchanging cards, here's mine. I live northwest of the city in Clarkstown." Our hands touched as he accepted the card and a spark of electricity shot through my fingertips. *Did he feel the same reaction too?*

Crawford studied the name and address on the cream- colored card with its border of pink magnolia blossoms. He tapped the card against his keyboard.

"You run a B&B ... Magnolia Blossom Inn?"

"Yes. Actually, I inherited the inn when Grannie died but I've lived there since I was a little."

"Mm-hmm. Sounds like a nice place. I'll have to stop by sometime."

"You're welcome any time."

I stood up, and we smiled at each other, feeling awkward and not sure what to do next. I hesitated then held out my hand to the detective.

"Well ... thanks for taking your time to speak with me."

"No problem, Miss Brooke. Like I said, I can't act without hard evidence. But it was nice meeting you," the detective said as he shook my hand, sending mixed signals, then ushered me out of his cubicle and toward the exit doors. I felt his earnest hazel eyes follow me as I stepped outside.

Could I really count on that guy to investigate Grannie's death? Despite being physically attracted to the handsome detective, I felt like I was on a fool's errand, and would get no support from the police. No ... I had to admit it, I'm on my own. I'm the only person who cares what actually happened to Grannie. Worse, I had no clue as to what I'd need to clear the debt hanging over Magnolia Blossom.

As I pulled into our yard, my cell phone rang. I picked up the phone from where it rested in the cup holder and recognized Lionel's number. For the first time that day, a pleasant surprise.

"Hey Lionel! What's up?" I asked as I parked the truck and climbed out. I slung my bag over my shoulder and walked toward the porch then dropped onto the swing. Luke trotted over to me for a nuzzle and pet.

"Hey girl. You up for some company tonight? Thought I'd pop over to work on the inn's web site."

I could hear papers rustling in the background and low voices. "Sounds like you're calling from work. How about you join me for dinner? I'll order pizza and we can discuss your ideas while we eat."

"Great. Should be there about six. That okay with you?"

"Perfect. See you then." I smiled as I ended the call. "C'mon Luke, bet you're hungry too."

Jumping up from the swing, I walked around to the back of the porch and entered the kitchen door. I dropped my bag onto the large farm table at one end of the kitchen then picked up Luke's empty bowls from the corner. Filling one bowl with fresh water, I set it on his mat then went to retrieve the bag of dog food from the cupboard. Luke greedily lapped up the cold water and waited eagerly for his bowl of food.

Tom shuffled into the kitchen as I stirred a can of beef and vegetables dog food into the dry mixture. Luke gave a bark of approval as I set it in front of him.

"Get everything you need?" Tom asked me, pouring himself a cup of coffee.

"Mm-hmm, I think so. Anything going on? Any calls?"

"Think I heard the phone ring but I was out in the hay loft in the barn, so I can't be sure. Did you know there are some boxes stored up there? Want me to get 'em down?" Tom asked.

"I'll check the answering machine. No, don't bother dragging those boxes out of the barn. I'll climb up and go through them there. If it's anything worth keeping, we can move 'em later."

"Whatever you say. Be careful climbing up that ladder; I'm not sure how stable that wood is."

"Okay." I carried my purse into the foyer where our reception desk sat adjacent to the front door. Picking up a pen and note pad, I pressed the play back button with its blinking red light and listened to the phone message. I jotted down the phone number and name before returning the call.

"Hello. This is Madison Brooke of the Magnolia Blossom Inn. Thank you for calling. How may we help you?"

"Oh, Miss Brooke, this is Myra Campbell. We wanted to book a three night stay for next week. I'm terribly sorry to call at the last minute. Do you have any rooms available?"

Flipping open the appointment book with its empty page staring at me, I was certain I could accommodate the woman and was glad to do it. "How many rooms will you need?"

"Just two. One for me and my husband and one for our son. We're visiting the university before Dennis enrolls for next semester and wanted to see the area," Mrs. Campbell explained.

"What days will you be arriving?" I mentally planned for the Jamison family to arrive this Wednesday and depart Friday. I thought I'd have enough time to turnkey rooms before these guests arrive plus the UVA students.

"Could we come in on Sunday and leave Wednesday? Dennis has an appointment with the admissions' office on Monday morning," she explained.

"I'm sure we can accommodate you. Our rooms each have a private bath and we serve breakfast in the morning from seven o'clock until nine. Refreshments are also served in the evening at seven. There's ample parking on the property. We are located on a farm so I must ask if anyone is allergic to dogs, cats, or chickens?" I recited our standard speech to new guests.

"It sounds lovely, dear. What time is check-in on Sunday?"

"You may check-in any time after two. Your rooms will be ready. I'll need a credit card for the deposit and to hold the reservation."

I repeated the card number back to her to confirm I had recorded it accurately and calculated the total cost with taxes then thanked her again for her call.

"We look forward to your arrival."

Finally, things were looking up. Between the cherry festival and the upcoming UVA graduation with families coming in from out of town to attend those events, maybe the inn will book more reservations. I'll take every dollar I can find.

Now to tackle those boxes in the loft before dinner and Lionel arrives. I quickly climbed the stairs to my bedroom, changed out of my nice blouse and pulled on another t-shirt before rummaging in the barn. I peeked into the guest bedrooms on the second floor on my way back downstairs for a quick inspection and made a mental note to add some fresh wildflowers to a vase in each room.

As I passed through the living room, the pile of ash in the fireplace caught my attention. I'd forgotten about that. Better sweep it out and clean the hearth before tackling the barn loft. Picking up a whisk broom and dust pan from the pantry, I returned to the hearth and dropped to my knees to gently sweep the burnt ash and tried not to create a cloud of dust. Poking among the gray powder, I notice fragments of paper that had not completely burned. Pulling a piece out of the dust, I found the bottom of a letter. The word *love* and the first initial of the author's name was visible— *W.* Unfortunately, the remainder of the name disappeared into the singed paper.

Who did I know with the first name beginning with W? My thoughts flew to Wallace Jackson. Was this proof that attorney Jackson was Grannie's past love? Is that why she was so upset with him? I tried to imagine him in that role.

I sat back on my heels and contemplated the scrap of paper with the curious signature. Tucking the bit of paper into my jean pocket, I carried the pan of ashes out to the kitchen and dumped them into the trash can. Using the hand vac, I made quick work of cleaning the residual powder that coated the brick hearth then put my tools away. My mind was still on the letter "W" as I walked toward the barn.

Chapter Ten

Ghosts: Past and Present

Tiny meows from scampering kittens drew me as I stepped into the barn. Mama Prissy basked in a shaft of sunlight while she kept a watchful eye on her brood. The kittens jumped and ran, skidded in the loose straw and tumbled over. I had to laugh as I watched them and couldn't resist picking up one of the furry balls for a cuddle. I stroked the kitten's soft fur and blew a puff of air to the top of its head. His little motor purred loudly, so adorable. Reluctantly, I placed him next to his mother and focused my attention on the loft ladder.

Slowly climbing the rungs, I stepped up onto the loft floor and glanced about the storage space. Five boxes were stacked to the right of the opening. Tom must have dragged them forward to make it easier for me.

The flaps of the cardboard boxes were tucked in but not sealed. I picked up one box and carried it closer to a bale of hay where I could perch while investigating. Maybe I'd find some family records and history to help explain my courthouse research.

Papers, envelopes, and scattered postcards filled the packing box. I picked among the papers, reading titles and skimming contents then set them aside as I assembled two piles. One I mentally designated business and the other one family. Anything concerning the farm or the inn I placed in the business stack.

A flat brown envelope contained military records for Grandpa Charles. Pulling out the government form, I read his name and Army rank, as well as the words honorable discharge at the bottom of the DD214 form. Digging into the envelope, I found more official documents that, on closer inspection, were copies of orders. The order sending him to Vietnam was among them. I never knew Grandpa had served in the war. Gosh, that must have been right after he and Grannie married in the early years of the conflict. My eyes searched for the date and found it— June 1965 until October 1966. Those were dangerous times.

In the bottom of the envelope, I found commendations written for a bronze star medal and a purple heart. Grandpa must have been wounded! He never spoke of his time in Vietnam and now I wondered if that was why he often wandered off and preferred the solitude of the orchard to being around people. Vietnam veterans weren't greeted with parades and laurels when they returned from the war. Even today, most 'Nam vets were denied the honor they deserved. My respect and love for my grandfather increased tenfold as I read his service papers.

Colorful postcards caught my eye as I reached into the bottom of the box. I saw one from Saigon and another from Bangkok, Thailand. The back of the cards contained only brief messages, one or two sentences, as if the author feared sharing too much with unknown readers handling the card during its journey through the public mail system. Grandpa must have traveled to Thailand on an R&R; his card mentioned seeing elephants.

"I remember running to the mail carrier every day praying for mail from Charlie when he was in Vietnam," Grannie said as she suddenly materialized in the barn loft. The stack of postcards magically shuffled back and forth like a deck of cards. One postcard appeared to float in the air as she studied it.

My hand flew to my throat; I'd never get used to her just popping in like that. "Why didn't Grandpa Charles ever talk about his time in the Army? I never knew he'd been in Vietnam."

"He'd put it behind him. Sometimes I thought he couldn't face the memory of buddies who never made it back when he did," Grannie said. In a burst of cold air, she was gone. The postcard fell to the floor.

Shaking my head at her disappearance, I placed the military records in my designated personal family history pile. Grandpa Charles should have been proud of his time in the Army. I certainly planned to preserve those records. Next, I opened a second box. The paperwork appeared to be more organized in this box. Neatly annotated file folders contained receipts and invoices for improvements done on the farm. I perused the documents and was about to close the box lid when a name jumped out at me ... Jackson. Why does that name pop up in all my family records? I wish Grannie had hung around long enough for me to ask her.

I set the box aside to carry it into the house where I could carefully read the documents in the privacy of my bedroom. Reaching for a third box, it tumbled over and spilled its contents onto the loft flooring. Black and white photographs, a few color shots, but mostly older images lay scattered at my feet. I picked up some of the pictures and studied the images of the old farm house and unknown people. Some pictures contained a date scribbled on the back ... wow, one said 1952. Scooping up the photos from the floor, I tucked them into an empty manilla envelope from the other box. I couldn't believe my eyes when I discovered old tin types among the modern photographs. They had to be at least a hundred years old, maybe older. Why would Grannie or Grandpa haphazardly stuff precious historic pictures of the farm into an old cardboard box?

Checking the time on my watch, I realized I needed to get ready for Lionel's visit. Digging around in the loft boxes raised more questions than answers. It would require more time than I could afford tonight, but tomorrow I planned to devote fully to identifying the images and the documents that I had found.

Tom entered the barn just as I began my descent down the rickety ladder. I had dragged the box containing the photos over to the top of the ladder at the opening in the floor, where I could inch it forward and drop it to the ground below.

"Hey Tom! Can you catch this? It's not too heavy."

"Yeah, go ahead. Just don't fall off that ladder in the process."

With my back braced against the ladder rungs, I slid the box toward me then released it. It fell right into Tom's waiting arms.

"Oh! Good catch. Thanks a bunch. I'm going to take that one back to the house."

"Right. I'll put it on the porch. I'm getting ready to leave for the day."

"Okay. Thanks Tom. See you in the morning," I said as I stepped off the bottom rung of the ladder and brushed off my jeans.

After washing up in the kitchen, I phoned in a pizza order then set the table for Lionel and me. A throaty engine sound drew my attention, and I ran outside to spot a sleek, new black Lexus pull into the yard. The SUV purred like a panther ready to pounce as it idled in place before the driver shut down the engine.

The driver's door opened and Lionel stepped out. He grinned from ear to ear at my expression.

"No way! Is that yours?"

"Like it? Just picked it up last week. She handles like a dream and get this, it's a hybrid—runs on a gas engine and electric. You won't believe the incredible mileage I'm gonna get and it's so fast," Lionel said proudly as he ran his hand along the smooth lines of the hood.

"Well, I'm impressed. It's beautiful. C'mon inside. Pizza should be here in a few minutes. I've got something I need to talk to you about."

"Okay. Lead the way."

We settled in at the large farmhouse table in the kitchen. I had set up my laptop on the table where we could work on the website together.

The folder containing the deed and my notes from the courthouse research was next to it.

"I hate to burden you with my troubles, but you're the only person I trust right now. With Grannie gone and my father off on another voyage, I don't have anyone to turn to," I said as I reached for the folder.

"Hey, I'm always here for you, no matter what. Why don't you tell me what the problem is and we'll tackle it together. We've faced challenges before, and we've always found a way through."

"My lawyer came over to have me sign the deed and I found a lien filed on our property. I went down to the courthouse to research the history of this land and all the deed transfers but I couldn't find any reference to the lien."

"What are we talking about here? How much is the debt?"

I paced the room. A dark cloud hung over me. Speaking about the debt, saying it out loud, made it real. I glanced up to see Grannie's ghost hovering in the corner, listening. The deed floated in the air. I grabbed it as I fidgeted with the folder of papers, then waved it to shoo Grannie and make her disappear before Lionel became suspicious. She wasn't taking my hint. Instead, she nodded for to me to continue. *Could Lionel see her?*

Lionel caught me looking about the room and raised an eyebrow, but didn't pursue it.

A knot tightened in my stomach. I stopped pacing and faced Lionel, "It's a whopping $50,000! If I don't come up with that kind of money, I could lose the inn and everything. I don't know what to do." I tried not to glance in Grannie's direction as I spoke.

"Okay, first thing ... don't panic. You're the historian and research specialist; you said you didn't find any lien filed at the courthouse? How can a lien be recorded on the deed and not be on file in public records? I think you need a second legal opinion other than Jackson's. Let me ask at the Center. We've got legal counsel there; I'll see if someone can advise you."

"Okay. That makes sense. As usual, whenever I'm spinning out of control, you're always there to ground me." The butterflies in my stomach landed but didn't completely fly away. I gave him a quick hug. Grannie looked on with approval. That reassured me.

The doorbell rang. Grannie's ghost popped into thin air like a soap bubble bursting. I ran to answer the front door. Pizza was here.

Carrying the large pizza box back into the kitchen, I placed it on the table. I grabbed two glasses and filled them with ice then opened the refrigerator for drinks, a Dr. Pepper for me and a Sprite for Lionel. We'd spent so much time together over the past years that I knew his preference.

"Let's eat while it's hot then maybe we can look at your website. Tell me what you like and what you don't, then I'll show you what I want to do," Lionel said as he reached for a slice of pepperoni and onion pizza.

I smiled at him, "Sounds like a plan."

My nerves eased just having him here. Lionel was my anchor with his calm, rational approach to any problem.

We finished our meal in companionable silence then I moved the pizza box onto the counter with its two remaining slices. Luke whined expectantly and nudged my leg.

"All right boy, here you go." I placed the slices in his bowl. With a gleeful bark, he woofed down the pizza in three bites.

Time to get down to business.

Logging onto the computer, I sat back while Lionel browsed through the website pages and studied its images and links. I watched as he moved the mouse between the pages and jotted down a few notes before commenting.

"Okay, what do you like about this site? Tell me how someone reserves their stay? Where do you list your promotions?"

"Hmm, I see what you mean. I like the pictures of the inn and the farm, but mostly it's a pretty basic site. Folks have to call us to book a room."

"That's all well and good, but most people don't want to take that much time or they might be cruising the internet at two in the morning to reserve a stay. If they can't book online, you're going to lose that customer."

Lionel opened my Word Press admin page and went to work. His fingers flew, and the mouse danced across the screen as he inserted links, buttons, and new landing pages while I watched in amazement.

"Alright, Maddie, let's dive into this website wizardry. First things first, we need a catchy slogan to drive customers to your page. How about '*Magnolia Blossom Inn: Where Southern Hospitality Blooms?*'"

"I like it! It's charming and captures the essence of our inn perfectly. Now, what about the home page layout? I want it to be warm and inviting." Lionel's excitement was contagious as I considered the marketing possibilities.

"Got it. We'll use warm colors, maybe some floral accents to tie in with the magnolia theme. We also need to highlight the unique charm and history of Magnolia Blossom Inn to appeal to a wider audience. People love staying at places with a story to tell."

"I found some historic family pictures today. Maybe we can include some on a history page about the inn."

Lionel's expertise made it look effortless as he navigated the web design tools and created the new home page, pulling in photographs of the inn during springtime and cherry festival season.

"You need a strong social media presence too. Are you on Facebook and Instagram? How about Twitter? We've got to direct traffic toward the website and booking."

"Well, Facebook but not Instagram, and certainly not Twitter. I've never bothered to get that involved. Should I be posting daily? I don't know if I have time to do that."

"At least keep your Facebook page current; perhaps post something new once a week, even if it's just a blurb about Luke or the trees in bloom. Get the idea? Okay. Let's set up an online booking system so guests can reserve their rooms with ease like I was describing. You tell me what your rates are and I'll list them next to each room description. No more phone tag trying to confirm reservations and folks can book late at night if they want," Lionel said.

I scribbled down the room rates next to each room name and slid the paper over to Lionel. He typed in the amounts next to each suite description.

"Great! I won't have to worry about missed calls and it will save me time too." I stared at the photo design spread on the home page "Wow, Lionel, this looks amazing! It's like our inn jumped right off the screen. I can practically smell the freshly brewed coffee and hear the birds chirping in the garden."

"That's the goal! We want potential guests to feel like they're already experiencing the charm and hospitality of Magnolia Blossom before they even arrive," Lionel beamed.

"It's perfect."

"Mission accomplished, my friend. Now, let's get this masterpiece live so you can start welcoming more guests through your virtual doors," Lionel said.

With a few more steps and tweaks, Lionel published the redesigned website. We high-fived each other, feeling proud of the accomplishment.

"I think this new site is guaranteed to attract more guests and generate some revenue for you. Maybe you can offer a couple special promotions or packages as a marketing tool."

"Thanks, Lionel. I could never have done this without you. I can't believe you got it all done in one evening. You're a computer wizard, for sure."

Lionel flashed me one of his big smiles. "I aim to please!"

"The cherry festival is coming up, perhaps it's not too late to put into play marketing promotions for the event. I've got to earn some money quick if I'm ever going to make a payment on that debt," I said.

The thought of the financial challenge hanging over my head burst my bubble and threw cold water on my momentary excitement.

Lionel sensed the shift in my mood as I walked him to the door.

"I get it, Maddie. It's a tough situation, but we'll tackle it head-on. We'll do whatever it takes to protect Magnolia Blossom."

"Thank you for always being there for me. You have no idea how much that means to me."

Lionel wrapped me in a brotherly hug while Grannie gazed at us from the second-story balcony. In that moment, the future didn't look quite as bleak as before. I could see a tiny flicker of light at the end of the tunnel.

Chapter Eleven

Guests

Bobbie Jo arrived on the same day as the Jamison family. Because I had to focus my attention on getting them settled, I could only direct my cousin up to the third floor and leave her to her own devices to haul luggage and unpack.

"Mr. and Mrs. Jamison, you'll be in our sunflower room number two and your daughters can share the daisy room number three that's right next door. There are twin beds in the daisy room. I'm sure the girls will be comfortable in there."

Tom and I carried our guests' luggage up the stairs as I showed them into the two bedrooms. A light breeze coming through the open windows ruffled the curtains and along with the ceiling fans, provided a comfortable temperature in both rooms. The daisy room delighted the girls with its pale blue and white feminine décor.

"Such a pretty room," commented Mrs. Jamison as she entered the pale yellow sunflower room with its muted black and white accent colors. "The flowers are lovely too."

I had carefully placed a vase of wildflowers in each room featuring the predominant named flower before their arrival.

"Thank you. I hope you'll be comfortable. Please let me know if there's anything I can do for you. Join us for breakfast at your convenience between seven to nine in the morning." I handed them the room keys and left them to settle in.

Dashing up to the third floor, I hurried to speak to Bobbie Jo. With a quick tap on her bedroom door, I opened it to find the room empty then turned at a noise in my room next door.

Luke lay in the doorway, a low growl rumbled in his chest.

"What's wrong boy?" I gave him a quick rub on the head. He barked as if to tell me something was amiss.

I walked into my bedroom to discover my cousin nosing around in the contents of the box I had brought up earlier.

"Looking for something?" I stood with my hands on my hips as I waited for an explanation of what she was doing snooping in my personal bedroom.

"Oops. That dog doesn't like me," she tried to change the subject as she pointed to the shepherd.

"What are you doing here?"

"I, ah, just wanted to see if you had some of Grannie's things. Sorry. I only meant to, you know, find something to remember her by."

Bobbie Jo's neck flushed a red color that rose from her collar bone toward her chin. It was a sure sign that she was lying. When we were kids, I could always tell by her flush that she told a fib. It would seem that she couldn't control the telltale reaction any more now than when she was a child.

"We have to share the bathroom, but that doesn't give you permission to snoop in my bedroom. What's in my room is private. Get it?" *Gosh, I sounded just like Grannie. Now I know how she felt.* "There are connecting doors on each side of the bathroom. When you're using the bath, just lock both doors for privacy. Also, I'm an early riser and need to be downstairs early especially when we have guests at the inn. I use the bathroom first." I shot her a stern look that proclaimed my message loud and clear.

"Got it. Your house ... your rules," Bobbie Jo said as she backed out of the room.

"That's right. Don't make me regret offering you a room here." Luke barked again, as if to punctuate my warning.

A gust of cold air announced Grannie's presence. *"I warned you. That chit will never change. She's up to something. I think I'll keep an eye on her."*

As I was about to answer her, she disappeared. Maybe Grannie is making good her threat and is spying on Bobbie Jo already. I chuckled to myself as I imagined Bobbie Jo's reaction if she ever saw Grannie's ghost.

As I assembled a tray holding a cookie assortment and beverages on the porch table near the rockers for the evening social time, a battered pickup truck entered the yard and parked. I watched two young guys jump out of the truck and realized my summer students had arrived. Luke barked their arrival and stood watch as they approached the house.

"Is this the, ah, Magnolia Blossom Inn?" asked the tall, dark- haired guy as he approached the porch. He kept a wary eye on the large dog.

"Yes it is. Are y'all from UVA?"

"Yes, máam we are," he answered. "I'm Noah Foster and this is my friend Sean O'Reilly."

"Maddie Brooke ... your hostess. Welcome to the inn." I held out my hand and shook each of theirs as I held the door open and gestured them inside. Luke sniffed the pair then trotted off, assured they meant no harm.

"Pleased to meet you. Thank you kindly for letting us stay here this summer," Sean said with a thick Irish brogue.

"We're happy to have you with us. You've arrived just in time to meet some of our other guests and to enjoy a small evening refreshment. If you'll each sign the register, I'll get your room key. You'll be sharing a room but it has its own private bathroom." I slid the register toward Noah and handed him a pen.

They each signed, then hefted their duffle bags over their shoulders and followed me up the stairs. Midway up, we met Bobbie Jo coming down.

"Well, hello!" she beamed as she looked the men up and down. She smiled coquettishly at each.

Sean returned her smile with one of his own, while Noah grinned knowingly.

"I like this place already," Noah said, and Bobbie Jo pretended to blush and giggle.

"I'm just about to get the guys settled into the ivy room number five at the end of the hall. The Jamison family are returning from their outing. Why don't you go down and play hostess? I've got the refreshments already prepared but they might want some coffee instead of the iced tea. I'll be down in a minute," I told my cousin, dismissing her and reminding her of her duties.

She nodded to me then batted her lashes at the men. "See you around." Her silky voice promised more.

I began to climb the remaining steps then turned and loudly cleared my throat to gain the attention of the two students who stood transfixed, watching Bobbie Jo's wiggling descent. At my harrumph, they hurried to follow, stumbling into each other. All I could do was sigh and roll my eyes. *Is this what I'm going to have to contend with ... Bobbie Jo and every available male in heat? I swear, she makes me feel like sixty-two instead of twenty-two. When did I become the house mother? Sheez!*

Ushering them into the muted ivy green and tan room at the end of the hall, I raised the pair of windows higher to allow the cool evening breeze to blow into the room. Noah and Sean each claimed a twin bed and dropped their gear on the floor.

"Sure is nicer than a dorm room," Noah remarked. He opened the bathroom door and peeked inside. "Real nice."

"Thanks. I think you'll be comfortable here. We serve breakfast from seven to nine each morning. You're on your own for dinner and supper. The front door is open throughout the day but I lock up at nine o'clock so if you're going to be out late at night, you'll have to ring the doorbell to get in." I handed them each a room key. "Come down for a snack when you're ready."

"Okay, great," Noah spoke for the two of them.

"Oh yes, one other thing ... no smoking inside the house. You can smoke outside if you want. Since you're going to be here all summer, I'd appreciate it if you'd keep your room picked up and I'll do the heavy cleaning and bathroom once a week. Deal?"

"We can do that. Thank you kindly," Sean said.

With a nod to them, I left and closed their bedroom door behind me. I hurried downstairs and out onto the porch as I heard Mrs. Jamison's voice.

"We had a wonderful tour of Monticello. Isn't it amazing?"

"Good evening folks. I hope y'all enjoyed your day. Please help yourself to the cookies. Can I or Bobbie Jo get you anything else to drink? Coffee or hot tea?"

"Thank you, this is fine. The girls like the lemonade and the sweet tea is perfect for us. I was just about to ask what other attractions are in the area. Perhaps you can suggest something?" Mrs. Jamison asked as she sipped her tea and reached for one of the decorated sugar cookies.

"We're honored to claim this region as home to three past presidents. Not only did Thomas Jefferson live in Charlottesville, but also James Madison and James Monroe. Their home estates are also nearby. Have you considered touring their homes?"

"Well no, I didn't know that. Can you provide us with more information?"

"Of course. Let me check on my desk. I believe I have a brochure from both Ash Lawn-Highland, which is Monroe's plantation, and also Montpelier— home of James and Dolly Madison. The Monroe plantation is only about three miles south of Monticello. Monroe and

Jefferson were great friends. Montpelier is about thirty miles north of Monticello. Madison's home offers limited touring hours, so check the web site or call ahead before you go but it's well worth seeing."

Mrs. Jamison grinned widely and clapped her hands. "Wonderful! We absolutely must visit them while we're in the area. Don't you agree, dear?" Her husband mumbled an agreement as she continued enthusiastically. "It will be such an excellent history lesson for the girls. Thank you, Miss Brooke, for suggesting them."

"Please, call me Maddie. I'm happy to provide you with the history of the region. History is my favorite subject and especially the Virginia colonial period. If you folks like a scenic drive, we are also very close to the entrance to the Sky Line drive. The view of the Blue Ridge Mountains is spectacular and there are numerous overlook places to stop and take great photographs."

Noah and Sean wandered onto the wide porch and munched on a couple cookies as they settled on the hanging swing. Bobbie Jo hastened to them, offering glasses of cool lemonade.

Their handsome looks, Noah with his dark hair and eyes plus Sean with his Irish red hair and deep blue eyes, were not lost on the Jamison tweens as they twittered and blushed while staring at the young men. Bobbie Jo threw a scowl in the direction of the oldest daughter, Mary, a budding thirteen-year-old.

I hastened to make introductions. "Mr. and Mrs. Jamison, Janet, and Mary, this is Noah Foster and Sean O'Reilly. Noah and Sean are both undergraduates at UVA and will stay with us this summer while the dormitories are being renovated. I believe you've already met my cousin Bobbie Jo Taylor. Please let Bobbie Jo or me know if you need anything to help make your stay with us more comfortable."

Everyone murmured greetings and exchanged pleasantries then the porch grew awkwardly silent. I felt at a loss. What would Grannie do?

"So, uh, Noah ... what are you studying at school?" I asked, in hopes of reviving the conversation.

"I'm pre-med. Figured medicine is where the money is so that's what my goal is— to be a rich doctor. Maybe I'll specialize in plastic surgery and charge lots of money for new noses or boob jobs." He laughed at his own joke. Mrs. Jamison cast him a look of disapproval and I think if she could have covered her daughters' ears with her hands, she would have.

I cringed, praying I wouldn't hear a similar outlandish answer when I turned to Sean. "How about you Sean? What brings you to America and what are you studying?"

"I'm majoring in economics, Miss Maddie. I hope to help my family when I return home." He smiled shyly at me and I exhaled a breath I hadn't realized I had held.

"I've dreamt of traveling to Ireland. What part of the Emerald Isle are you from?" Mrs. Jamison asked politely.

"My family lives in a small village in County Cork. Ah, tis a lovely place and I miss my mum and sisters. Being the sole lad in the family, it's my responsibility to take care of the women folk. I plan on starting a business, putting my degree in economics to use when I get home."

"I wish you luck in your senior year of school then. Being from Ireland, I don't suppose you'd like to share any Irish tales or songs for our amusement?" I asked, as I spotted the gleam in his eye.

"Well ... seeing as how you're asking, I don't mind if I do," Sean said in his marvelous Irish brogue with a chuckle, then produced a harmonica from his pocket. He played a lively tune, stopping between notes to teach us all the words of the ditty so we could sing while he played. By the end of the song, we all applauded and held our sides from laughing uproariously.

Noah rose as if to stretch his legs, and I spotted the incline of his head toward Bobbie Jo. She jumped up too and started down the steps.

"Let me show you around while it's still light," she addressed her remarks to Noah and they nonchalantly walked off toward the barn.

Sean raised an eyebrow and gave me a wink while I cleaned up the tray of glassware and empty cookie plate. He lent a hand, holding the door open as I carried the dishes into the kitchen.

The Jamison family wandered into the house and made their way up to their rooms. I could hear the girls still singing the Irish lyric as they went. Overall, I think everyone enjoyed a pleasant night.

Chapter Twelve

Thief Amidst Us

A delicious cinnamon scent wafted through the air as I carried a large pan of thick French toast to the dining room table. Tom had created a breakfast treat for our guests with his decadent French toast soaked in a rich egg milk mixture flavored with vanilla and liberal amounts of cinnamon then fried to a golden brown and served with real maple syrup. The Jamison family entered the room and took their seats as I placed a platter of crisp bacon and a bowl of fresh raspberries and blueberries before them.

"Orange juice, everyone? There's brewed coffee on the sideboard and a pot of hot water for tea, if you'd prefer." I smiled at my guests as I served glasses of juice to Mary and Janet.

"This looks wonderful," commented Mrs. Jamison as she spooned berries on top of her French toast.

"I hope y'all enjoy it. This dish is one of Tom's specialties. Where are y'all off to today?" I asked.

"Mmm, we thought we'd tour those estates you mentioned and then perhaps visit Michie's Tavern."

"I'm sure you'll enjoy that. The tavern is a perfect example of colonial life."

The Jamison's finished their meal and were just leaving when Noah and Sean stumbled into the dining room. Both boys still appeared to be half asleep.

"Top of the morning," Sean greeted as he slid into a chair. "Smelled too good to stay in bed."

"Yeah, good morning," Noah mumbled as he poured himself a mug of coffee and eyed the food on the table.

"Serve yourself the French toast and I'll get another plate of bacon," I told them as I pushed open the swinging door to the kitchen. Tom handed me a fresh batch of bacon.

"Here you go fellas," I said as I placed the plate in front of them. "Have y'all seen Bobbie Jo this morning?"

"Mm-hmm, ran into her in the hallway. Think she was going into the girls' room to make the beds," Noah said.

Pouring them each a glass of juice, I left them to their meal and hurried upstairs. Bobbie Jo came out of the daisy room as I rounded the landing.

"Thought I'd get the beds made while they're out," Bobbie Jo commented.

"Thanks. I'll take care of the parent's room. You go ahead and grab some breakfast for yourself then clear the dishes after Noah and Sean finish. Okay?"

"Yeah, okay. What do I have to do after that?"

"Maybe you can show both the guys around and just kind of keep track of them for me today until they find a routine."

"Guess I can do that," she said with a smile. I knew I had played right into her hands with the perfect assignment.

I watched her skip downstairs as I turned to the sunflower room and entered to make the beds and freshen the bathroom for the Jamison's. Peeking into the girls' room, I checked on Bobbie Jo's work and was pleased to see she'd done a neat job making the beds and had even straightened up the bathroom and hung clean towels. Moving down the hall, I opened the door to the ivy room to see what needed to be done.

To my surprise, both guys had made their beds, not precisely tucked corners, but neat enough. Wet bath towels were on the floor of the bathroom, so I scooped those up and hung new ones before returning downstairs. I'd have to start a load of laundry before collecting eggs from the henhouse.

The dining room had been cleared and Tom had finished loading the dishwasher when I retrieved my egg basket from the kitchen.

"Great breakfast, Tom. Everyone gobbled it up."

"Thanks. Your cousin is outside with those guys. I'd keep my eye on that girl," Tom said as he nodded toward the sound of Bobbie Jo's giggle coming from the barn.

I nodded as I left and walked toward the henhouse. Maybe I better peek into the barn first, just to see what's going on. Their voices sounded muffled and more distant now.

Prissy ran between my legs as she dashed out of the barn. I stood in the doorway wondering what had gotten her dander up. The trio of kittens romped in the corner of an empty stall. All appeared to be well there. A shaft of straw floated down onto my head and I heard shuffling from above in the loft.

"Bobbie Jo! Are you up there?"

Muffled giggles met my inquiry then I saw the top of Noah's head peer over the edge of the loft. I set my basket down and climbed the ladder up to the loft; halfway up I stopped when I was high enough to see into the space. Bobbie Jo's face flushed red, and she fumbled with the buttons on her blouse as I stared at her. Noah only grinned.

"What's going on? Where's Sean?" I asked and felt foolish for asking. It was obvious what was going on. *She's making me feel like a house mother again for delinquent girls!*

"I think Sean is in the orchards. Yeah ... he might be there. Did you want something?" asked Bobbie Jo in an innocent voice that didn't fool me one bit.

I turned my head to start back down the ladder when I noticed the box I had left in the loft lay open. Someone had rifled its contents. Pausing, I glanced back at the wayward couple.

"You've no business poking into the boxes stored up here. Do I make myself clear? Noah, as a guest of the inn, I expect you to mind your own business and manners and respect our property. Bobbie Jo, I believe we have already talked about this."

"Who died and left you in charge?" Bobbie Jo complained in a strident voice then her voice dwindled into a mumble as she realized just what she asked. She had the presence of mind to at least appear embarrassed.

I made my way back down the ladder and grabbed the basket. Storming out of the barn, I stopped to take a deep breath and control my emotions. That gal made me so angry and then she threw salt on the wound by bringing up Grannie's death. Allowing her to stay here was a mistake. Grannie was right.

After collecting the eggs, I returned to the barn to confront Bobbie Jo but didn't see her there. However, I caught sight of Noah crawling on his hands and knees in one of the stalls. How odd.

"What are you doing?" I asked.

He backed out of the stall and jumped up. As he brushed off the loose straw from his pant leg, I spied his hand slipping an object into his pocket. What had he found?

"Oh hey, just playing with one of those tiny kittens. You don't mind, do you? They're awfully cute."

Somehow I doubted that's what he was actually doing, yet I couldn't put my finger on why I didn't trust him. Two little kittens scampered out of the stall and ran toward Prissy. Maybe he was playing with the cats. *Was I becoming paranoid?*

"What? No, I don't mind if you play with the kittens. Like I said though, I'd prefer you don't go back up in that loft. The ladder's not safe anyway."

"Yeah, well … sorry." He mumbled then turned his back to me and strolled out of the barn.

I watched him depart and shook my head. The hairs on the back of my neck prickled. What was it with that guy? What did he put in his pocket? I walked into the stall that Noah had been in and looked around; it was empty except for a small bale of hay and loose straw. Nothing.

⁂

It was early evening and Tom had left for the day as I prepared a tray of crackers and cheese cubes for serving with wine as that night's refreshment. I had completed the arrangement and was just beginning to carry it outside when I heard a car drive in. Luke immediately barked and ran into the front yard. The dog stood in front of the steps guarding the house.

Setting down the tray on the porch table, I was surprised to recognize the handsome Detective Crawford getting out of the police cruiser. He stood a moment and gazed around the property before striding toward the front of the house as he spotted me standing on the porch. Luke growled at the stranger. Crawford stopped at the canine's warning.

"Want to call off your dog?" Crawford spoke in an even tone, not wanting to sound threatening.

"Sorry. Luke ... heel! Good boy." I patted the side of my leg and Luke trotted over to me as docile as a lamb.

"Hello Ms. Brooke, er, nice place," Crawford said as he slowly advanced toward the house.

"Detective Crawford. What brings you out this way?"

He strode up the steps, stopping a few feet from me, keeping his eye on the German shepherd. "There's been a report filed. One of your guests has claimed to be robbed. Do you know anything about this?"

My hand on my throat, I could only nod no, as I slowly sank onto a rocker. "Who? When? Oh my goodness."

"Do you have a Mary Jamison staying with you?"

"Yes, she's the daughter of one of our guests. This is the first I've heard of anything wrong. When? I mean, good gracious …"

"I'd like to speak with Mr. and Mrs. Jamison to learn more and perhaps see the girl's room," Crawford said.

"Of course. They just got back from touring all day. I haven't seen them since breakfast. I can't believe any one at my inn would steal. What was lost?"

"The girl claims she left a pair of gold earrings and a matching gold chain necklace on her dresser and now they're gone. Her father called the station and reported the loss because of the value of the items."

"No one has been in her room except to make the beds since this morning." My thoughts flew to my cousin Bobbie Jo. Would she have taken the items? Noah and Sean were late for breakfast, could one of them taken it?

Crawford saw the doubt written on my face. "What are you thinking? I can see you've thought of something."

"No, it's silly. It couldn't be. Perhaps if we helped search the room; maybe they fell off the dresser. I trust my staff but I certainly don't want my guests to feel violated in my home. Theft is serious. That kind of reputation could ruin a B&B."

"So again, I ask you, who were you just thinking of? Like you said, this is serious business and a possible felony."

"Let's go inside," I suggested as Noah and Sean with Bobbie Jo walked up the side steps onto the porch. I shot a glance at the trio and wondered if one of them could have taken the jewelry.

The detective stood in the living room. I noticed he checked out the furnishings, the antiques, and valuable artwork on the walls. He had to realize how unlikely someone associated with the inn would commit burglary, but then again, it wouldn't be the first time in his line of business. He waited as I gestured him to follow me up the stairs.

I knocked lightly on the door of the sunflower room. Mrs. Jamison opened the door and frowned at me as I stood next to the officer.

"I understand your daughter may have lost some jewelry. This is

Detective Crawford. He'd like to speak with you both. I'm sure we can solve the problem. May I help search in Mary's room?" I asked.

"You can search but I doubt it will do any good. Someone on your staff has stolen my daughter's jewelry," snarled Mrs. Jamison. "We'll be leaving in the morning and don't expect a positive review!"

"If I might have a minute of your time, máam, I just need a few more facts," Crawford said as he pulled out his small notebook and pen. He stepped into the room as I knocked on the daisy room next door.

"Your not going to find anything in there," Grannie whispered to me. She hovered on the upper stairs.

I quickly looked behind me, insuring we were alone in the hall. "Why? What do you know?" I hissed.

"I told you it was a mistake letting that chit stay here. Now look at the trouble she's brewing." In a poof of cold air, she disappeared, leaving me to stare after her as Mary opened the bedroom door.

"What do you want?" the young girl sneered.

"Oh, I, uh, understand you are missing some jewelry and I wanted to ask if I could help you search for it. I'm terribly sorry if there's a problem and would like to help solve it." I tried to smile sweetly at the rude teen.

Mary grudgingly opened the door wider and allowed me to come in. Her sister stood by the window and watched as I crawled on the floor and ran my hand under the dresser then under the bed. Nothing but a dust bunny missed during cleaning.

"I don't know why you're putting on a big show; you know you won't find my gold earrings and chain ... you stole them," Mary accused me. She stood with clenched fists and a defiant look in her eye.

My anger began to simmer, but I tamped it down as I replied to the girl's accusation. "I'm sorry you lost your jewelry, but I assure you I did not steal it. I promise you I'll sort this out." I turned to exit the room and bumped into the very solid chest of Detective Crawford.

"Oof!" His hand grasped my elbow to steady me as we collided.

I raised my eyes to his and in that fraction of a second, a spark flickered and threatened to ignite. He must have felt it too, because he released his hand as if it had been burnt.

"I, uh, searched under the furniture in case the items had fallen to the floor, but I found nothing," I sputtered.

"Uh huh, I'd like to speak with the other guests and staff," Crawford said.

"Of course. We have two college students staying with us as guests and my cousin who is helping out. Other than my cook and handyman, Tom, I'm it. No other staff."

"Must keep you busy," he commented as we made our way back downstairs.

Hearing voices on the porch, we went outside to confront Bobbie Jo and the guys.

"I'm Detective Crawford. I'd appreciate a moment of your time. I'm investigating the theft of some gold jewelry. Would you give me your name please and tell me your whereabouts today from about eight o'clock this morning until four this afternoon?"

"Sean O'Reilly. I'm a student at UVA. Guess I came down for breakfast about eight-thirty, then I went for a walk in the orchards for an hour or so. Later I went into town with Noah."

Noah glanced at Bobbie Jo then answered the officer. "Yeah, uh, Noah Foster. I'm also a UVA student staying here this summer. Sean and I came downstairs together, and after breakfast I hung out in the barn for awhile then went into town. Guess we got back about five."

Bobbie Jo sidled up to the detective and smiled seductively then frowned when she didn't get a response. At my cough, she threw me a glare before identifying herself. "I'm Bobbie Jo Taylor and I'm sort of working here this summer helping my poor cousin. I was working upstairs doing maid duties until nine o'clock and then I was permitted to eat my breakfast. After that, I gave a tour of the farm to Noah and Sean before we all drove into town. I had shopping to do while the guys hung out."

"Did you enter the Jamison rooms?" asked Crawford.

"Well, duh, of course I did. Who do you think made the beds and cleaned up the bathroom after those girls made a mess?"

Crawford scribbled a few notes then raised his eyes to Bobbie Jo. "Did you notice whether or not the gold jewelry was present in the room?"

"Gee, I don't know. I don't recall."

"All right. That's all for now." He snapped his book closed then stepped off the porch.

I followed him to his car. Luke stood at my side.

"I'm going to file this report with the robbery division, Ms. Brooke."

I nodded. "All right Detective Crawford. How come someone from your robbery division isn't here now? Why you?"

"I, uh, saw the Magnolia Blossom name on the report and thought I'd check it out myself. And it's Allen."

"Please, call me Maddie. I can't help thinking the pieces will turn up. I plan on continuing to search for them. I hate that this has happened. I'll have to refund the Jamison's room costs as compensation, of course. Will this incident show up in the newspapers or some public record? It'll destroy the inn's reputation."

A compassionate look passed over his face as he listened to me. "You've got my card and number. Call me if you find anything. I can't promise, but I'll do what I can to keep this quiet."

"Thank you, Allen."

I stood in the yard and watched him as he slowly maneuvered his car and drove back down our lane.

Chapter Thirteen

Lies

If I had to spend all night, I was determined to locate that missing jewelry. I slowly climbed the stairs and headed toward the third floor, where I might speak with the one person who could help. Standing outside Bobbie Jo's bedroom door, I listened for sounds of her presence. Nothing. All quiet.

Slowly turning the doorknob, I slipped into my old bedroom then turned on a dim lamp. I shook my head in dismay as I looked at the clutter in Bobbie Jo's room. Discarded clothes lay where they fell. Her bed was unmade and a damp towel draped our connecting bathroom door.

"Grannie? I need your help. Please show yourself." I spoke in a hushed voice, fearful someone on the floor below might hear me.

Opening dresser drawers, I poked among my cousin's belongings, searching for the missing jewelry. A flurry of movement on the curtains and a puff of cold air announced my grandmother's appearance.

"Try looking under the mattress. I saw her hide something under there early this morning while you were in the guest rooms," Grannie whispered.

I turned from the dresser and moved to the bed. Lifting the

mattress, I ran my hand underneath on one side then moved to the other side of the bed and did the same. Success! My hand came out from under the bedding clutching a folded washcloth. Placing the bundle on top of the bed, I opened it to find the missing gold earrings and necklace.

"Oh my goodness! What should I do? The jewelry has to be returned to Mary Jamison but should I admit Bobbie Jo stole it? Won't that guarantee bad publicity for the inn?"

"Tell the Jamison's you found it in the vacuum sweeper. As long as they get the jewelry back, that's all that matters. I warned you about letting Bobbie Jo stay here. Let me deal with her; I'll cure her of having sticky fingers," Grannie suggested with an eerie cackle.

"Hmm, I hope they buy that story. The important thing is to make everything right with them. I'll deal with my dear cousin later," I said.

Checking the time on my watch, I went down to the second floor and tapped on the sunflower suite door. It was only a little after nine; I hoped they hadn't gone to sleep yet.

Henry Jamison opened the door then turned to call his wife.

"Louise! That Madison woman is here again."

Missus Jamison pulled her cotton duster closed as she approached the open doorway. I waited until she stood before me then I held out my hand with the missing jewelry still wrapped in the washcloth. I thought it would look more plausible that way.

"I found your daughter's jewelry. After searching all the rooms and not finding anything ... uh, it occurred to me that the items might have fallen to the floor and been accidentally sucked up in the vacuum cleaner when we swept earlier. So, I dumped out the vacuum bag and sorted through the dirt. I'm relieved to say I was right. Please accept my apologies for the mishap."

Louise Jamison snorted as she grabbed the jewelry from my hand. "That's a tall tale if ever I heard one."

Her husband stepped forward. "What does it matter? You've got the stuff back and maybe the next time, Mary will be more careful with her belongings. Let the matter drop."

My gaze flicked to the husband then back to the wife. "Naturally, Mrs. Jamison, there will be no charge for your rooms as compensation for your inconvenience."

She made a noise in the back of her throat before closing the door in my face.

Humph, that went well! I trudged downstairs to straighten up and perform my nightly lock up routine. Luke pattered in from the kitchen, droplets of water clung to his snout where he'd guzzled his water bowl.

"Hey boy, where is everyone, hmm?" I rubbed the top of his head and scratched behind his ears.

Luke barked once and shook his head as if answering my question. A throaty giggle in the night air drew me to the front porch. I stepped outside and silently closed the screened door behind me. Bobbie Jo cuddled next to Noah on the wide swing. Sean sat on a rocker at the other end of the porch with his iPhone in hand. Evidently, he preferred to distance himself from the amorous pair.

"Bobbie Jo, I need to speak with you. Now!"

She untangled herself from Noah's arms then shot me a hateful glare before following me back into the house. I led her into the dining room where we would be out of earshot.

"What? Can't I have some personal time?" Bobbie Jo whined.

I stood with my hands on my hips and returned her angry glare with one of my own. How dare she put me in the position of lying to a customer and losing income for the inn!

"I just returned the gold jewelry to the Jamison's and had to apologize for their loss." I saw her eyes widen in surprise, but she wisely chose to stay silent. "Yes, that's right, I found it hidden under your mattress. What kind of mischief are you brewing? What do you have to say for yourself?"

"Nothing! That Mary was a spoiled brat. I saw the way she flirted with Noah. She deserved to lose the jewelry. Her rich mommy and daddy will buy her more."

Her spiteful words left me speechless. Clenching my fists, I sputtered and paced the floor in front of her before stating my ultimatum.

"Now you listen to me and listen close. I've covered your butt this time, but if you ever do anything like that again, I swear I'll call the police and have you arrested. I'm only offering you a chance to make amends now because you're family. Don't push the issue. One more slip up, one little infraction, and you are out of here quicker than you can spit. I expect you to be on your best behavior and that includes not sleeping with the male guests," I growled. My voice shook with pent up emotion and frustration.

Bobbie Jo flung open the door and stormed outside. The screen resounded against the siding, which added fuel to my anger. I began to follow her across the yard and into the barn for a second confrontation but halted at the sound of Lionel's car pulling into the yard.

Lionel got out of his SUV and walked toward me as I turned my back on the barn. He stopped and scrutinized my face.

"Whooee, you look madder than a wet hen!"

"Huh ... you don't know the half of it," I said through gritted teeth with a fleeting look toward the barn.

"What's wrong?" he asked. He linked his arm through mine and we headed toward the house.

"C'mon in and I'll get us some drinks. How about a glass of wine? I could sure use one. What are you doing out here, anyway?" I asked as we entered the kitchen.

I grabbed a bottle of zinfandel and a pair of glasses. Flopping onto a kitchen chair, I poured us both a healthy amount then took a large swallow of my wine.

"Slow down girl; tell me what's happened."

"Oh Lionel! I could just kill my cousin." I glanced over my shoulder then lowered my voice before continuing. "She stole some gold jewelry from one of my guests. The police filed a report and everything, then I had to comp their rooms to persuade them to not bring further charges against me and the inn."

"Did you get the jewelry back?" Lionel asked then took a healthy sip of his wine.

"In a manner of speaking ... after I retrieved it from under my cousin's mattress and gave it back to the guest. I lied and told them the vacuum cleaner sucked it up by mistake. The wife didn't believe me but the husband insisted she drop the issue and they're leaving in the morning. Can you imagine the damage to my reputation if that woman posts a bad review and robbery claims?"

"Wow! No wonder you were mad. What are you going to do now?"

"Well, I just gave my cousin a warning and told her she's on thin ice with me if she pulls another stunt like that. I really should kick her out but with the cherry festival starting next week, and the additional guests that have booked, I need her help. I'm not sure it's worth it, though."

"Stand your ground. That's all you can do when dealing with someone like her. Hey, I came out here to see if you wanted to speak with Lee Warner tomorrow. He's the center's legal counsel I told you about. I explained your problem from what you shared with me and he said he'd be interested to check into it."

"Oh gracious, I'd forgotten all about it, what with the drama going on around here. After these folks leave in the morning, I can drive into town. Would he be free around one o'clock? I might be able to come in the morning if the Jamison family leaves early."

"Lee told me he was free most of the day but if you can get in before eleven, that might be best. At least he could have the rest of the day to start his research."

"Okay. I'll plan on doing that. Bobbie Jo will just have to take over doing the turn key on those two rooms and clean up after breakfast. Serves her right."

"I'll send him a text and let him know you'll be in to see him. Make sure you bring that deed with the lien and maybe your research from the courthouse too. Anything you think will help."

"Thanks Lionel. I owe you one. If I have to pay that lien, I'm never going to scrape together enough money if I keep throwing away rental income. What a mess!"

I leaned back in my chair and silently drank my wine while I tried to calm myself. Lionel draped an arm around my shoulders and gave me a quick hug.

"You've got this. Don't worry. Tomorrow will be a better day," he said.

"God, I hope so."

Lee Warner shook my hand and instantly put me at ease when I entered his office at the African-American Heritage Center the next morning. He was a tall man with warm coffee- colored skin and short-clipped gray hair like President Obama. When he spoke in a deep mellow voice, I instantly associated him with the actor Morgan Freeman.

"Lionel tells me you recently lost your grandmother and inherited her bed and breakfast inn along with some worries. I'm sorry for your loss but perhaps I can help ease some of your problems," Attorney Warner said. He took his chair and waved Lionel and me into two others facing his desk.

Unlike the stiff-backed chairs I had sat in at the police station, these were comfortable upholstered seats meant to relax an occupant. I studied the well-appointed office with its golden oak wood furnishings and burgundy paisley wallpapered walls before turning my focus back to the man patiently waiting in front of me.

"Thank you for seeing me. I'd really like your legal opinion on a debt that was added onto the deed for my inn. I've got a copy of it here," I said as I reached across his desk and handed him the paperwork. I sat back in my chair while he read the document.

Lionel nodded to me and I smiled at him weakly. Opening my note-book, I flipped to the page with the deed lineage that I had researched.

"When Attorney Jackson had me sign the new deed, he told me that by doing so I was acknowledging the debt on the property. I went to the courthouse in Charlottesville and spent hours going through the Grantor and Grantee books researching the past transfers of this property," I said.

"And what did you discover? Was this lien recorded with the clerk of courts?" asked Warner.

"No, it was not. I found no record of it at all. How can that be? Here's a list of owners for this property with dates of transfer going back to 1830 when the land was first purchased by the Brooke family. I only found one entry where a parcel of land had been divided and sold in 1935. Incidentally, that sale went to someone named Jackson. Coincidence ... or the same family as Wallace Jackson?"

"Hmm, I see. Sounds like you're implying charges against Attorney Jackson. I don't suggest you make any false accusations on a member of the bar, Miss Brooke. However, I think this lien on the deed is highly irregular and bears looking into. If you want me to do that, I will."

I squirmed in my seat with downcast eyes, feeling like my school principal had just chastised me. He was right, of course. Raising my eyes to him, I apologized. "I'm sorry. Yes, I'd appreciate your help. I know I shouldn't make wild accusations but my research kept uncovering the Jackson name intertwined with Brooke over the generations. I can't help but wonder if this lien is some type of plot to acquire the rest of the property. Steal it away from the Brooke family."

"Give me some time. Lionel and I will dig a little deeper and see what we find. Meanwhile, take my professional advice and do not voice any accusations against Wallace Jackson unless you want a lawsuit on your hands for defamation of character."

Chapter Fourteen

Mishaps

When I returned from Charlottesville, I peeked into the vacant guest rooms and found the beds made up with fresh linen and the bathrooms scrubbed clean. It both surprised and pleased me that Bobbie Jo had followed directions and accomplished her tasks. Maybe I had been too hard on her. No ... what was I thinking? She stole from that girl out of spite, and that was wrong. I needed to keep reminding myself of that and not go soft.

Returning downstairs, I entered the kitchen and noted the dishes had been loaded into the dishwasher and two washed skillets sat on a drying mat on the counter. The only noise in the room came from Luke gobbling the bowl of food I had set out earlier. The house was strangely quiet, and I hadn't seen or talked to Grannie since yesterday and the jewelry caper.

Entering the foyer, I checked messages on the answering machine then logged onto the computer and signed into our new website. The appearance of the home page made me smile. Lionel's artistic design had created a welcoming presentation of Magnolia Blossom Inn. Clicking on the reservation page, I was delighted to find several pending bookings for the next weeks during the cherry festival. All I needed to do was review the guest information and room requests before clicking on the confirmation button. My goodness, could it get any easier? What a marvel! I needed to thank Lionel again when I saw him.

Strolling outside, I noted the battered pickup truck belonging to Noah and Sean parked in the side lot. No one sat on the porch or strolled the grounds. Luke trotted out of the kitchen door and ran across the yard into the orchard. Voices carried on the air from that direction. Maybe Bobbie Jo and the guys were there.

Walking toward the barn, I decided to bring down that last box of records and store it under my bed — out of harm's way and snooping eyes. Until I learned if that box held any significant documents, I better keep control of it. I just didn't trust Bobbie Jo to leave things alone. She was up to something.

Prissy and her kittens lay on a bale of hay where the mama cat attended to their hygiene by licking them clean. She had her work cut out for her. I smiled at the adorable kittens as I filled a bowl with fresh water and scooped some cat kibble into another. With four mouths to feed now, I'll have to remember to put out an extra dish of food.

As I climbed the loft ladder, I heard a car pulling into the gravel lot. With one hand on the rung above my head, I paused and turned to look out the barn door at the new arrival.

"Hello! Anyone here?" asked a nasal voice in a heavy Yankee accent I recognized.

"In the barn!" I shouted. Putting my foot on the next rung, I stepped up higher on the ladder when the upper rung that I held snapped. I tumbled backwards with a scream. "Help!"

Allen's strong arms caught me just in time before I cracked my head on the hard cement floor. However, twisting my foot on the ladder, I experienced a wrenching pain in my left ankle.

"Are you all right?" he asked as he cradled me against his broad chest.

My eyes fluttered and I moaned in pain as I attempted to move. His arms drew me closer and I decided I very much liked the position.

"It happened so fast. Guess that old ladder broke."

"What were you doing up there?"

"I wanted to carry down a box from the loft."

"Anything broken?" Allen asked as he gently ran his hand over my arms and legs. I winced when he touched my ankle. "Tender? You need a doctor to look at that. I don't think it's broken but it might be sprained."

The ankle in question throbbed and appeared to be swelling under skin turning a lovely purple color. I reached into my back pocket and pulled out my cell phone. Dialing Dr. Houser's number, I explained to his nurse about the accident.

"Thank you. I'd appreciate it," I said into the phone. "The doctor is out making his rounds but his nurse will get hold of him and send him here. He's one of those old-time physicians that still makes house calls to his regular patients," I told Allen.

The detective shook his head in wonder. "Amazing. Thought that practice ended half a century ago."

"Suh, y'all forgetting where you are." I batted my eyelashes dramatically as I informed him in my best southern drawl.

Allen laughed and slid me off his lap onto a nearby bale of hay. "You okay to sit here while I have a look at that ladder?"

"Of course. Tom has been warning me that the wood on that ladder was rotten. I should have heeded his words."

Grannie's ghost hovered above the barn loft. She appeared to be interested in what the detective was doing. I wish I could have spoken to her, but with Allen within earshot, I couldn't. *Why didn't she warn me about the broken ladder? Where was she when I needed her?*

Allen walked over to the ladder and picked up the broken piece of wood laying beneath it. He examined the rung in hand then climbed up a few steps to peer at the empty space.

"Hmm. This looks like the wood has been cut. The break is too even, not ragged from simply breaking off."

He climbed back down and sat next to me. "Would anyone want to harm you?"

My face expressed my shock as I raised my eyes to him. I slowly shook my head no, even as my mind leapt to question if my cousin could be so angry with me as to see me harmed. Could Bobbie Jo have tampered with the ladder?

Allen stood up then bent toward me. "Put your arm around my neck and I'll carry you back to the house."

I reached up and draped my arm across his wide shoulder; my fingertips couldn't help but touch the fringe of dark hair above his collar. He easily carried me as if I weighed nothing at all, and I admit I was content to let him do so. I felt like one of those heroines in a romance novel.

"Where to?" Allen asked as he climbed the steps onto the wraparound porch. Luke trotted over to his side and whined.

"Here's fine. I'll sit on the rocker where I can put my foot up on that stool. Thanks."

He lowered me carefully onto the chair. Our faces came together; I lowered my eyes anticipating his kiss, but my fancies burst as he abruptly straightened. I heard a car door slam. The doctor had arrived. *Thanks, Doc, perfect timing.*

"Well Madison, what seems to be the problem?" The gray-haired physician asked as he slowly mounted the steps.

A low growl rumbled in Luke's chest as the doctor approached. The dog's reaction surprised me and I rubbed his back to settle him down. Luke quieted but stayed by my chair, ever vigilant.

"I fell in the barn, Doc. Think I twisted my ankle."

"She fell about seven feet off a ladder in the barn. I got to her in time to keep her from hitting her head but I think her foot got tangled in the ladder." Allen filled in more details for the doctor while I tried not to wince as the doctor slipped off my sandal and prodded my swollen ankle.

"Mm-hmm. I see. I want you to follow RICE ... rest, apply an ice pack every two to three hours, compression, and elevation. I'm going to wrap your ankle in an elastic bandage for compression of that swelling. Stay off that foot and keep it elevated," the doctor advised me.

I sat meekly under his ministrations while thinking of all the things I needed to do to prepare for cherry festival and guests due to arrive tomorrow. How am I going to stay off my foot? Impossible.

"How about some ice?" the doctor asked.

"Um, I keep a blue ice pack in the kitchen freezer," I said.

Allen jumped up. "This way?" He entered the house and found the kitchen. I heard the noise of him moving stuff in the freezer before he found the ice pack buried under packages of frozen vegetables and meat.

"Here you go," Allen said as he handed the ice pack to the doctor, along with a linen dish towel from the kitchen.

I was glad he had thought of wrapping the ice pack in a towel so it wouldn't touch my bare skin. That was thoughtful, but then it seems I was just getting to know the many sides of Allen Crawford.

Leaning back in my rocking chair, I watched as Wilbur Houser conferred with the detective who, I mused, had stepped in and taken charge of my care.

"Call me if that ankle feels worse, otherwise, I'll check on you in a couple days," Doctor Houser said as he stepped off the porch and headed toward his car.

"Thanks, Doc," I called after him and waved.

Allen sat on the rocker next to me; Luke sniffed his hand then butted his head against the detective's knee, prompting him to scratch the shepherd's enormous head. *Hmm, Luke seems to have accepted the Yankee. I wonder why he reacted so menacingly to the doctor?*

"Um, you never said ... what brought you out here?" I asked.

"Henry Jamison called the station and canceled the robbery report. He said the jewelry had been found and he didn't want to press charges. I thought you'd appreciate hearing that kind of information from me personally. Although I didn't expect to rescue a damsel in distress, I'm glad I was here."

"Thank you for saving my life. I'm really glad you came by when you did. I hate to think what would have been my fate without you. My hero." I smiled warmly at him and liked the way his face took on a boyish expression and blush at my words of praise.

"Um, well uh, happy to be of service máam."

"Would you like something to drink? Can I get you a plate of peach cobbler? Tom baked a cobbler yesterday for today's dessert; it's in the refrigerator."

"Thanks, but I don't think you better be walking on that foot. You heard the doctor," he said.

Just as I was about to protest and get up, Bobbie Joe and the boys approached the porch.

"What happened to you?" Bobbie Jo demanded as her glance took in my bandaged ankle propped on a cushion. She eyed the handsome detective then shifted her gaze elsewhere as he studied her guilty face.

Chapter Fifteen

Consultation

Allen Crawford stood with one foot on the top step as he prepared to leave. I think he lingered, waiting to hear my cousin's comments. Watching him, I knew he scrutinized the two young men with Bobbie Jo. An eyebrow raised, and he frowned as he sized them up. It was obvious the men interested him and had triggered his cop's intuition. I couldn't imagine why. I admit Noah impressed me as someone hiding secrets and up to no good, but Sean seemed honest enough and trusting. Hmm, it would be interesting to know if Allen's impressions matched mine.

"Maddie fell off the loft ladder in the barn. Any of you been in there lately? I don't suppose you'd know how a rung on the ladder got sawed off?"

"Why, detective, it sounds like you're accusing us of tampering with the ladder. Can we help it if Maddie dear is clumsy?" Bobbie Jo taunted.

Leave it to Bobbie Jo to push my buttons. She knew her words would rile me. "Well Bobbie Jo, no matter how the accident happened, I'm going to be laid up and you will need to take on more responsibility for the next few days. We've got guests arriving tomorrow so you're going to be busy."

I watched her gasp and sputter then glance at the three men studying her reaction. Suddenly, she was all meek and mild ... the picture of a caring cousin as she turned to me. "Of course. You know I'll do anything I can to help— we're family. I'm sure Sean and Noah wouldn't mind lending a hand too. Won't you, guys?"

"Uh, yeah, guess so," Noah mumbled.

"Happy to help, Miss Maddie. Don't you worry none," Sean piped in.

Between the two, I rather thought I could count on Sean more than Noah. As for Bobbie Jo, I didn't trust her as far as I could throw her. The next couple of days should prove interesting.

"I've got to be going. I'll call you tomorrow to see how you're managing," Allen said, with a last nod to me and a warning look at the other three.

My cell phone rang as I hobbled into the kitchen then collapsed onto a chair. I had to take a deep breath and wait a second to recover from the exertion of bouncing on one foot.

"Hello?" my voice sounded like I had run a mile.

"Maddie? It's Lionel. Did I catch you out jogging?"

I laughed into the phone. "No, far from it. Sorry. I'm just a bit winded from hopping around the kitchen. What's up?"

"Hopping? Like a rabbit? Do I want to know why you're playing jack-rabbit in the house?" asked Lionel with a chuckle.

"Long story. I sort of fell and sprained my ankle and now I can't walk on that foot. It's a mess but I'll manage somehow."

I could hear the concern in Lionel's voice as he rushed to ask, "Do you need anything? Sorry, here I am mocking you and you're really hurt. Is there anyone there to help you? I was going to drive out to discuss your deed research, but if you're not feeling well ..."

"No, no ... please come ahead. I'd love to hear what you learned. Come by any time; I'm not going any where."

"Okay. I'm gonna give Lily a call and see if she can come with me, maybe grab a pair of crutches so you don't need to hop."

"That would be great. If Lily can't make it, can you bring the crutches with you any way?"

"Sure thing. See you later," Lionel said as he ended the call.

I leaned back in my chair and breathed a sigh of relief. It would be good to hear what Lionel and Attorney Warner unearthed on that lien. Plus, I urgently needed to bounce some ideas off my friends. Their advice and calm reasoning were what I craved now, along with a private chat with Grannie. Where was she?

"Does it hurt much, baby girl?" Grannie asked with a whoosh of cold air as she materialized next to me in the kitchen corner.

Jumping at her sudden appearance, I hissed at her, "I swear Grannie you're going to give me a heart attack popping in like that!" I glanced furtively through the window at the trio sitting on the porch, fearful they'd overhear our conversation. Lowering my voice to a whisper, I inquired, "Where've you been? Why didn't you warn me about the tampered ladder? I thought you would protect me."

"I'm a ghost, not an all-seeing super power. I can't be in two places at once. Sorry, but I was keeping an eye on that Noah. He's up to something; I could feel it in my bones, if I had any." She chuckled at her own joke.

"Allen thinks someone deliberately cut that ladder rung knowing I'd be climbing up to the loft. I could have been hurt worse, even killed, if Allen hadn't caught me. I'm scared, Grannie."

"I'll keep watch over you," she said before she vanished.

Lionel and Lily arrived an hour later. Lionel carried in a pair of crutches as Lily rushed to my side.

"Let me see that ankle. Have you been putting ice on it and elevating that leg?" Lily asked as she unwrapped the bandage and prodded the swelling with her fingertips. "Well, at least Houser didn't put you in a cast. I have to agree with his assessment of the injury." She re-wrapped the bandage on my ankle then filled a food storage bag with ice cubes and placed the cold pack on my leg. Lily returned the thawed blue ice pack to the freezer.

"Try these out for size," Lionel suggested as he produced the pair of crutches.

"I never thought I'd be happy to use something like this, but it beats balancing on one foot." I removed the ice pack and stood, grasping the crutches under my arms and practiced taking a step forward with the stick bearing my weight. "Let's move into the living room where we can talk," I suggested.

Lionel carried the bag of ice and followed me into the secluded room. He rushed to set a pillow on the coffee table for me to rest my foot as I leaned back on the sofa. Lionel sat next to me while Lily took the side chair.

"First tell me what happened to you then I'll show you what Warner and I found on the lien," Lionel said.

Both of my friends waited quietly for me to begin. Lionel clasped his hands together while Lily studied my face.

Speaking in a low voice, "I almost don't know where to begin, Lily, but it's been crazy around here since the funeral. My cousin Bobbie Jo moved in to lend a hand while she supposedly works on an art project." I snorted. "I haven't seen her lift a paint brush yet. I've also got two UVA students boarding for the summer and currently the inn is booked with guests for the upcoming cherry festival. The other day Detective Crawford paid me a visit because one of my guests reported some gold jewelry stolen." I paused at Lily's gasp and Lionel nodded his head.

"Was the jewelry really stolen?" Lily asked.

"Yes ... by my cousin. Can you believe it? She took it from a teenage girl that had eyes for Noah. He's one of the students and Bobbie Jo has laid claim to him. Anyway, I found where she had hidden the earrings and necklace then returned them to the owner. Luckily they dropped the charges but I've been so distraught worrying about the inn's reputation if that kind of story got out. I could just strangle my cousin for pulling a stunt like that. Lionel knows, he was here right after it happened."

"I don't blame you for being angry. Did you confront Bobbie Jo?" asked Lily.

"Yes, I did. I made up a story to the family about the missing jewelry but I told Bobbie Jo if she ever pulled a stunt like that again I'd turn her over to the police."

"Okay, so how did you hurt your foot? What does the jewelry theft have to do with that or am I missing something?" Lionel asked.

"Honestly, I think Bobbie Jo deliberately tried to hurt me. Allen ... I mean Detective Crawford, stopped by to tell me about the charges being dropped and thank goodness he did, because he caught me as I fell from the broken ladder in the barn. He told me someone had tampered with the ladder; it didn't break because of rotten wood."

"Hmm, Allen is it?" Lily picked up on the one item that interested her.

"Um, yeah, he told me to call him Allen. He's really a nice guy. But you're missing the point. I think my cousin tried to get back at me. She knew I had to climb that ladder to reach some boxes that were stored in the loft. Grannie had put several boxes of inn records, old family photos, and grandfather's military papers up there. I went through some of that stuff the other day and had one more to retrieve when the ladder broke."

"Wow! After all that, I'm surprised you're letting her stay here. I'd have booted her out on her ear," Lionel huffed.

"Believe me, I wanted to but I'm short-handed and now with this stupid sprain, I need her help more than ever." I took a deep breath. "Enough of my woes, what did you find?"

Lionel opened a folder filled with a copy of the property's deed and other documents. He sorted a couple pages until he pulled out the first one to show me.

"Warner and I retraced your research at the courthouse and found the same deed that you did, minus the suspicious lien. Then we concentrated on the lien itself, so I did a deep dive on the internet for the name listed on your deed copy and found it's linked to a corporation. Searching for the corporate owners led me to another company with its director recorded in Richmond. The shell company is just that, an empty shell with no assets, just a name and tax identity to shield its link to the corporate entity that filed the lien. Really was an amateur job; I could have hidden the identity much better and so deep no one would have uncovered it." Lionel grinned proudly and shot us each a look, expecting to hear our agreement. Disappointed by our silence, he continued, "Guess whose name links with this daisy chain?"

I shook my head. I had my suspicions, but that's all they were. Not facts. "Don't keep me in suspense," I whispered. I glanced anxiously out the bay window and around the room, hoping no one was listening to our conversation.

"How about Wallace Jackson? Just as you suspected," Lionel said, as he sat back with a smug look on his face.

"I had a feeling. I've found the Jackson family name on old records that link his family with my Brooke ancestors and there was even a transfer of acreage between the Brooke and Jackson families back in 1935. Also, wait until you hear this, I found love letters that were written to Grannie when she was a young woman, signed by someone with the first name beginning with the letter W." Now it was my turn to sit back and gauge their reactions.

"Really? Why would a lover only sign an initial?" Lily asked.

"Um, they weren't. I mean, the love letters got burned and the only thing left was part of the signature. But that W could stand for Wallace, don't you think?"

"What ... you think he's like a jilted lover or something?" asked Lionel in disbelief.

"Maybe. He could be. Grannie told me, I mean ... I remember her saying, she'd known Wallace Jackson a long time. Besides, he kept asking me if I wanted to sell the property and implied I'd lose it if I didn't pay off the debt. Do you think he could want this property bad enough to commit murder?"

Lily looked at me askance. I could see the wheels turning in her head, recalling our conversation about ghosts.

"Whose murder? You've lost me again," said Lionel.

"Grannie's murder. What do you think I've been talking about? She didn't die of old age, that's just poppycock. I think someone killed her and I'm trying to find out who," I insisted.

"That's a heavy accusation, Maddie. Do you have any proof? I agree Jackson might plot to swindle your land, but murder?" Lionel asked.

Lily reached for my hand and held it between her own comfortingly. "Maddie, I know you're still grieving and you've had a shock, but you aren't thinking clearly."

She spoke to me like I was one of her disturbed patients. I yanked my hand free and glared at the pair of them.

"You're my friends. I expected more support from you than this. I am not losing my mind nor do I need your condescending bedside manner." My voice had risen. I swallowed hard to calm my outburst then lowered my voice to a loud whisper as I continued. "I'm telling you that Grannie's death is suspicious and I think it's part of a plot to gain ownership of Magnolia Blossom and its fifty acres of prime real estate. Do you have any idea what this land is worth? Well I do. Attorney Wallace Jackson has been acting strange and even tried to cajole Grannie into selling. When she wouldn't, I think he took it further."

"Don't jump to any rash conclusions. Let me dig a little deeper and see what else I can find out. Okay? If it's any consolation, Warner advises you not to pay that lien. He thinks it's a fraudulent scheme," Lionel said and hugged me.

"I'm here for you too, Maddie. All I ask is for you to be careful," Lily said and squeezed my hand.

I folded my arms across my chest, mumbled, and stared out the window as my friends took their leave.

Grannie hovered above me. Her whispered voice only added to the silence of the room.

"Give them time, Maddie. It's a lot to digest. Your friends care for you, don't be too hard on them."

With a poof and a ripple of air, she was gone.

Chapter Sixteen

Plots

Dusk turned to night as I sat alone pondering the information Lionel had found. I knew my friends meant well, but I couldn't shake the nagging feeling that both of them were just humoring me. They didn't believe my statement that Grannie had been murdered. No one did, without any evidence. But how was I supposed to conjure evidence out of the blue? Wasn't the fraudulent lien on my property enough proof? That had to be Wallace Jackson's doing; Lionel proved that. I was dead certain of it.

A timer turned a light on in the kitchen. I blinked at the infusion of light seeping from the kitchen doorway. My corner of the living room and the rest of the house remained dark. The night air filled with the sweet scent of magnolia blossoms, and the soft hum of cicadas provided an evening song. Reaching for the crutches, I tried hobbling up the stairs when I heard voices whispering outside. I paused, sat back down, and held my breath. The porch floor boards squeaked as somebody stepped lightly, but the old house spoke in its own voice. Straining to listen, I recognized Sean's Irish brogue and then Noah's deeper tone drifting through the open windows.

"I think I've stumbled upon something profitable," Noah said in a loud whisper, colored with excitement. He stood near the porch railing, then peered over his shoulder into the inky night to assure himself they were alone.

Sean leaned toward him, intrigued. "Oh, you have, have ya? What's your latest plan? I know you're always hatching something."

Noah grinned, his eyes danced with anticipation. "I found an empty syringe in the barn. And I've got a plan to turn it into some quick cash."

Sean's eyebrows shot up in surprise. "A syringe? Do ya think someone has been doing drugs? What are ya going to do with that?"

Noah and Sean moved further down the porch. Noah's voice dropped lower, for Sean's ears alone.

"I'm tired of always being the loser. It's time for me to be a winner and come out on top. All my life I got the fussy end of the lollipop, but not now. Think I finally found a sure thing. I'm

going to blackmail Bobbie Jo. She told me she's part of the family that owns this place. Means she's gotta have money. I'll tell her I found evidence that could link her to something ... unsavory. I'll threaten to take it to the police if she doesn't pay up."

Sean's eyes widened, a mixture of doubt and concern on his face. "What's she doing working as a maid if she's got money? Noah, your idea is risky. What if it backfires? Sorry Mate, I don't think I want any part of that."

Noah waved off the concern with a cocky grin. "Trust me, Sean. I've got this all figured out."

Wishing I had heard more of the conversation, I listened to their footsteps as they approached the front door. I shrank back into the shadows of the living room to avoid being seen. A syringe ... maybe that's what Noah pocketed when I saw him in the barn. Could he be right? Was someone doing drugs at Magnolia Blossom? Who ... Bobbie Jo or Tom? It was difficult to believe, but why else would a needle be found in the barn?

Cherry Festival began the next morning with a parade down Main Street in Clarkstown and the crowning of the festival beauty queen, Miss Cherry, at the picnic that followed. Tom and I watched from the sidelines as the crowd cheered the beauty queen. The local high school band marched behind the festival float; their horns and trumpets blasting. We enjoyed the sights as long as we could then hurried back to the inn.

We got home just in time to welcome the Campbell family's arrival to the inn, plus a huge crowd of locals that came every year to pick cherries from the orchards. This year was no exception. Tom had set up a small stand with a scale and stack of cardboard containers to weigh the pecks of sweet cherries, which we sold for three dollars a pound. In the henhouse's cool shadow, I perched on a wooden chair next to the scale and money box to spend the busy afternoon greeting neighbors and newcomers.

"Thank you for coming. Enjoy those sweet cherries," I said to one customer.

"Hello Madison, dear. Pity you didn't have an entry for this year's pie contest. We missed you at the picnic," Mrs. Ginther oozed as she sidled up to the stand and placed her cherries on the scale.

Giving her a slight smile, I spoke through gritted teeth, "Have a nice day."

The festival committee held a special cherry pie bake-off contest every year. Prize-winning blue ribbons were awarded at the picnic. This was the first year that Magnolia Blossom Inn did not enter a pie. Grannie's homemade cherry pie won several past ribbons, but without her, there was no entry this season.

I sighed as I thought of the contest and how Grannie had enjoyed the cherry picking season on the farm. Maybe next year I could try to follow her recipe and bake a pie.

Tom approached my booth with a glass of iced tea in his hand. "Hey, thought you might want a break. I'll take over here. Why don't you go into the house and eat some lunch. Rest up a bit and elevate that foot."

I gulped the cold drink, quenching my thirst, then carefully adjusted the crutches under my arms. "Thanks Tom. Sounds like a good idea."

I limped toward the house then abruptly halted, staring at the open barn, alerted by Luke's angry barking. Tom and I exchanged worried frowns at Luke's fierce growling. Pivoting, I attempted to hurry toward the structure. Tom ran five steps ahead of me.

As I entered the barn, Sean cowered before Luke. It appeared Sean had attempted to climb a horse stall partition. The dog growled menacingly and blocked his exit from the enclosure. Noah lay motionless on his stomach, his legs bent in an awkward position and his right arm stretched away from his body. My mind raced as I viewed the scene. Had the two men argued? What happened? Was Noah unconscious ... or worse?

Tom crouched near Noah's body, checking for a pulse. He rose then scanned the vacant barn.

"Don't touch anything," Tom warned.

"I'll call 9-1-1. We need an ambulance," I said in a trembling voice. Holding my cell phone in a shaking hand, I tapped in the emergency number and gave the dispatcher my information. This can't be happening! It felt like déjà vu.

Tom moved toward Luke to calm him. "Easy boy. I've got this. Stay Luke!"

The German shepherd shook his big head then lay on the floor with paws outstretched. His vigilant gaze stayed on Sean. Luke appeared at rest but could jump to attention in a second. Sean gulped and shifted his eyes from the watchdog to the man standing before him.

"I didn't do anything. I swear! I found Noah on the floor just like that," Sean pleaded.

As we waited for help to arrive, I kept scanning the barn for a sign of Grannie's presence. I yearned to question her and learn what she had witnessed or what clues might link to her own death. The nightmare never ended.

Doctor Houser sauntered into the barn, his black leather bag in hand. Sirens sounded coming from the road and a police cruiser skidded to a halt outside the barn entrance. Luke growled again at the doctor's appearance.

"Tom, you better check on the stand and any pickers still on the property. Maybe we better send everyone home," I suggested.

Detective Allen Crawford held up his hand to halt Tom as he walked toward us. "I'm gonna need to speak with anyone on the property. Why don't you gather folks in the parking lot?"

Tom nodded then glanced at me; I shrugged, acceding to the detective's authority.

"Want to tell me what happened?" Allen asked.

"I don't know, really. We're celebrating the cherry festival today and we've had people in the orchards all day picking cherries. I got up to go into the house when Luke began barking loudly in his alert voice. Tom and I both headed to the barn and we found Noah on the floor and Sean over there in the corner. Luke was keeping Sean at bay. We didn't touch anything. I called for an ambulance. That's it."

Doctor Houser knelt on the floor, examining the patient. He shook his head as the detective watched. "Dead. Help me roll him over onto his back."

The two men carefully rolled Noah onto his back. His left arm had been trapped under his body. I gasped when I viewed the body. A hypodermic needle protruded from the veins in the crook of his elbow on the left arm. Accidental drug overdose or murder? Was Noah a user? I didn't know him well enough to speculate.

I watched as paramedics hurried forward with a stretcher. My mind tried to absorb the horror of the moment while part of my thoughts puzzled over how fast Doctor Houser had arrived on the scene. How did he know to come? My call into 9-1-1 requested the ambulance from the medical center, but they just pulled in minutes behind the doctor.

Detective Crawford snapped pictures of the scene and Noah's body with his i-Phone camera then removed the syringe and deposited it into an evidence bag. He knelt and searched the ground near the body; his hand cautiously feeling through the loose straw. Slowly rising, he nodded to the paramedics.

"All right, you can take the body now. I want an autopsy performed by the medical examiner of Albemarle County."

"Gotcha," replied one medic, as they carried Noah's lifeless body out of the barn and slid the gurney into the back of the ambulance.

We quietly observed the door shut and the squad slowly departed from the yard.

Crawford approached Sean. His expression conveyed the seriousness of the situation as he pulled his notebook from his pocket.

Sean gulped visibly as he faced the officer.

"I'd like you to come downtown with me. I've got a lot of questions for you to answer," Crawford said in a no-nonsense tone of voice.

Poor Sean. I saw his face blanch as he gulped again. His Adam's apple bobbed up and down in his throat. He was hiding something; his nervous reactions gave him away. I wondered if it had anything to do with the conversation that I had overheard the night before.

A uniformed policeman entered the barn and approached the detective. Crawford acknowledged the officer with a nod. "Place this man in the back of the cruiser, he's going into the station for questioning. Hold him there until I get there. Next, I want a forensic team in here. Bag anything that seems out of place. Be careful ... there may be additional needles lying about." He handed the officer the evidence bag. "I want that analyzed. Treat it as the murder weapon."

"Yes sir."

My thoughts were still puzzled by what my eyes had seen, but what my brain couldn't quite grasp. What was it that niggled at me? I felt like an important memory clung to the back of my mind and eluded me.

Moving to stand next to Doctor Houser, I blurted out the burning question on the tip of my tongue.

"Who called you? How did you get here so fast?"

The doctor coughed then lifted his shoulder in a half shrug as he admitted, "I heard the call on my scanner and recognized the location. I had planned to stop by and check on your ankle so I was close by. Headed here as quick as possible."

"Uh huh. I see." Was his explanation too pat? What was he really doing here? First Grannie's death and now Noah ... these deaths were making me distrust everyone and every motive.

A low growl rumbled from Luke as he sidled closer to me and placed his large body between me and the doctor's in a protective stance. It would seem even my German shepherd distrusted the kind doctor.

Chapter Seventeen

Questions

Sitting on the cushioned porch swing, I observed Detective Crawford make quick work of questioning the people rounded up from the orchards. He lingered on the handful of people that were nearer the barn at the time the emergency vehicles arrived. I scanned the yard and realized one person was missing. Bobbie Jo. She was normally in the thick of any activity, and her absence seemed odd.

Grannie occupied the other end of my swing. She sat listening to the conversations going on around her, taking it all in. I kept waiting for her to voice an opinion, but she remained strangely silent. It seemed no one acted in character today.

Luke rested by my side as the commotion in the yard dwindled. Tom stayed busy cashing out the quantities of cherries picked as the day came to an abrupt end. Perhaps we'll have some folks return later in the week. I hoped so; it would be a shame to see the cherries rot or go to the birds if left unharvested. One more revenue stream we counted on had now been crippled.

Allen approached the porch. Luke barked once in greeting and allowed the man to pet him. I noticed Luke didn't seem to worry about my safety in the policeman's presence. He trotted off into the kitchen where I heard him slurping his water and crunching on kibble.

I smiled at the detective. "Have a seat," I offered, then feared he might sit on top of Grannie on the swing.

Allen chose a rocker across from me; he paused and drew a deep breath before choosing his words. "Tell me again what you saw when you found your grandmother and why you think her death is suspicious."

My eyes widened and eyebrows raised at his words. I hadn't expected that. "Does this mean you believe me? Um, do you think Noah's death has anything to do with Grannie's? Noah and Sean weren't even staying here yet when she passed away." *I'd love to know what Grannie thought of his inquiry.*

"Look. I don't believe in coincidences. I have to question when two people die in the same place and one other person barely escapes a serious injury; they've got to be related somehow. So, tell me again about your grandmother."

He leaned forward with his elbows resting on his thighs and his fingers intertwined. His penetrating, gold-flecked hazel eyes studied my expression as I relived the moment in my mind.

"He's a good-looking young man, for a Yankee. Polite too," Grannie whispered to me.

Now, she chose to talk? I could only pray that my face did not mirror my reaction to her words. Unfortunately, I did not have a poker face and often regretted my lack of emotional control.

"Well, um, let's see. Grannie and I had breakfast then went about our normal morning chores. I had fed the hens in the pen and our cat Prissy, while she was going to collect the eggs. I returned to the house to start laundry. Grannie had stayed in the barn; I heard her talking with Prissy, our cat. At least, I thought that's who she spoke with."

"Who else was on the property that day?" Allen asked.

"Tom was here. He was in the kitchen cleaning up after breakfast.

We had one couple that we served breakfast to earlier before they checked out. That's it. No other guests, just the three of us."

"Okay. Then what happened?"

"I, um, wondered what was keeping Grannie so long so I went back outside. When I entered the barn, she was laying on the floor. I rushed to her side and checked for a pulse then felt for signs of an injury or blood, but I didn't find any." My voice trembled in the retelling.

"It's okay, baby girl." Grannie whispered, comforting.

Allen reached for my hands, clasping them in his larger, warmer ones. "I'm sorry. I know this is difficult for you. Did you hear any sounds ... any indication that someone else may have been in the barn?"

I closed my eyes as I tried to picture the scene in my mind. "The only thing that I can remember is Luke growling. I couldn't see where he was but I could hear him."

"I've seen for myself how the dog reacts when he feels a family member is threatened. Is it possible that he might have pursued someone who killed your grandmother? Perhaps that person escaped out of the barn before you came in or hid somewhere within the barn. You said there were no signs of casualty to her body. What did the doctor say was cause of death?" Allen asked, as he considered all possibilities.

I made a snorting sound that ended in a hiccup. "Doctor Houser pronounced her dead from natural causes. He said it was old age. I don't believe it and you wouldn't either if you had known the woman."

"I understand. You have every right to feel skeptical. Sure wish there had been an autopsy," Allen voiced in exasperation.

"Tell him I had marks on my throat. Someone had there hands around my neck before I felt a pinch," Grannie interjected.

I wondered how to explain Grannie's comment without outright lying. Maybe a little fib wouldn't hurt. I swallowed and cast my gaze at the field of wildflowers.

"There may have been some faint marks on her neck, like a hand print. Though the doctor didn't mention strangulation, so maybe someone just held her. Is that possible?"

"Why wasn't that included in the original report?"

"Um, uh, maybe because no one asked and the doctor signed the death certificate as natural causes? I was never questioned about what I saw."

"Will you be all right staying out here? This place is rather isolated."

"Of course, I'll be fine. Tom is here and my cousin Bobbie Jo plus we still have guests staying in the inn. I can't abandon them. As you said, Luke will protect me. My ankle is getting better and I should be off these crutches in another day."

"I don't like leaving you alone, but if as you say, there are other people on the property, I suppose it will be okay."

"When you're done questioning Sean O'Reilly, will you release him? Can you call me if he needs a ride back to the inn? I honestly can't see Sean harming Noah. He's a gentle soul."

My thoughts turned to the conversation I had ease-dropped on between Noah and Sean. I frowned as I debated whether to mention it to the detective. Unfortunately, my traitorous face gave me away.

"What are you thinking? I can see worry in your eyes," Allen said as he studied my face.

"Um, I suppose I should have mentioned this earlier, but I, um, overheard Sean and Noah discussing a scheme to get money. It was late at night and they were outside on the porch and didn't know I was nearby. Noah told Sean he had found something 'profitable' ... I think that was the word he used. He might have mentioned blackmail and I heard Sean say he didn't wany any part in it. I'm not sure; it was difficult to hear their voices." I wrung my hands as I waited for the impact of my confession.

"This makes all the difference in the world. It's obvious that Sean and Noah must have argued and Sean attacked him. Thank you for telling me. Did Noah say what he had found?"

"Yes — a syringe in the barn."

Now it was Allen's turn to express surprise on his face.

Waiting on Lionel to answer the phone, I drummed my fingers on the table as I listened to the persistent ringtone. Finally, I heard a breathless answer.

"Hello?"

"It's happened again!" I announced in a tremulous voice.

"Maddie? What's happened again?" Lionel asked, clearly perplexed as to what I was talking about.

"A dead body, that's what! Noah, one of my student lodgers, is dead. It was horrible," my voice sounded shrill to my own ears.

"Okay, slow down. When did this happen and did you call the police?"

"Yes, of course," I said in an impatient tone. "We found him around noon today. Police and ambulance have been here and gone. He was jabbed with a needle. I saw it sticking out of his arm. It was gruesome."

"Wow! Drug overdose, do you think?" Lionel asked.

"I don't know; I don't think so. It reminded me so much of how I found Grannie. Can we get together?"

"Yeah, of course. How about Lily? Let me call her and we'll coordinate a time. Can I pick you up later?" Lionel's reasonable voice took command.

"Okay. Yes, I think I need to get away from here for a little while. Shoot me a text with the time and I'll be ready."

I ended the call with Lionel then hobbled into the foyer to check the answering machine and computer messages and try to calm down. Anything to distract me from Noah's death. Conncentrating on the computer screen, I almost jumped out of my skin when Bobbie Jo suddenly spoke from behind me.

"What's going on?" she asked.

I spun in my chair to face her as I demanded, "Where have you been?"

Bobbie Jo flicked her hair and straightened her shoulders as she looked at me defiantly. In a whiny voice she explained, "Upstairs in my room. I was tired since I'm the only one doing any work around here now. I made up the Campbell rooms then laid down with a splitting headache. Guess I fell asleep."

"Uh-huh, and the sirens from the police cars and ambulance didn't wake you. Am I supposed to believe that fairytale?"

"Believe it or not ... your choice. So what's the big deal? Did you say police cars and an ambulance?"

"Noah is dead. Sean has been arrested or at least the police escorted him to the station for questioning. They consider him a person of interest. And you slept through all of that? Amazing." I shook my head at the sheer absurdity of her statement.

Bobbie Jo sank onto a chair and slapped a hand over her heart. I watched her face take on a look of tragic grief and thought Bobbie Jo had missed her calling. She should have been on the stage.

"Oh my! Poor, poor Noah. How did he die? He was such a sweet guy," she lamented, with tears shining in her eyes.

I rolled my eyes and looked upward to the heavens, or at least to Grannie's ghost hovering near the ceiling, for answers.

"She's lying," said Grannie.

"The police will probably want to question you later. I'm going out in a little while, so you're on your own for the evening," I told her. "The Campbells check out in the morning. I can help make up their rooms after they leave tomorrow."

"Fine!" Bobbie Jo stated belligerently as she turned in a huff and stomped into the kitchen.

I heard the back door slam as a text notification jingled on my cell phone. Glancing at the short text, I read Lionel's message that he'd be here in thirty minutes. Perfect. Just enough time for me to get upstairs and change clothes.

Chapter Eighteen

Person of Interest

"Where're we going?" I asked Lionel as I hopped into his Lexus. He laid my crutches across the rear seat.

"We're meeting Lily on her evening supper break so I thought the Panera close to the hospital would be best. Lily can walk over and not waste time driving."

"Okay by me." I leaned back into my seat and watched the scenery zip by as Lionel drove toward Charlottesville.

"How you holding up?" he asked with a quick glance before turning his attention back onto the road.

"I dunno. Okay, I guess. There's just been so much that's happened since Grannie died. I feel like the world has turned upside down and I'm supposed to know how to correct it. In reality, I haven't a clue."

Lionel made a noncommittal noise in the back of his throat as he headed toward campus. He smoothly maneuvered the SUV into a parking space, then jumped out to rush around to my side and helped me out of the car. I balanced on my crutches as I slung my purse over my shoulder. With a nod, we started toward the entrance just as Lily met us. As usual, Lily had walked at a fast clip from the hospital a block away.

"Hey guys! How's that foot doing, Maddie?" asked Lily with a quick hug and greeting.

"It's getting better."

Lionel held the door open for me and Lily. The smell of rich coffee and cinnamon pastries filled my nostrils as we entered the shop. We approached the counter to place our orders while Lionel scoped out the room for an empty table. He spotted one against the window wall and pointed.

"Okay, I see it. Order me a strawberry poppyseed chicken salad with sweet tea, please. As much as that cinnamon coffee cake is calling my name, I'm gonna resist. I'll be glad to get rid of these awkward crutches; they're such a bother in a crowded room. I better get out of the way and go hold the table for us," I said.

Lily scanned the menu then decided upon the Greek chicken salad with iced tea. She gave her order to the clerk.

"Mmm, everything looks good. Think I'll get the chicken cobb salad, and if you ladies don't mind, I'll have a slice of that cake," said Lionel. "You go ahead. I'll pay for these and they'll bring 'em over when they're ready."

"Thanks."

I waited until Lily and Lionel were both seated before broaching the topic that had brought us all together.

"Noah's death was not an accident or suicide. I don't mind telling you, I've got the willies. It's too much like Grannie's death. What's going on? Do you think someone is trying to scare me out of my home? Force me to sell?" My whispered voice trembled as I spoke.

Lily squeezed my hand in comfort. "We're here for you and no one is going to force you out of your home. We won't let that happen. Will we, Lionel?" Lily tried to reassure me.

The waitress arrived with a tray of salad bowls and drinks then placed them on the table. We waited silently until she finished and returned to the kitchen before speaking. My fingers drummed on the table as my anxiety grew.

"I've been thinking of all the facts I've uncovered ... the family history. I've come to a conclusion. I know who killed—" my phone rang, interrupting my words. Detective Allen Crawford's name on my caller ID surprised me. "Hello?"

"Madison, it's Allen. I've got the tox report back on the contents of that syringe. Noah was poisoned with ethylene glycol, basically, antifreeze. Common ... available anywhere, but lethal if ingested by the human body and more so if injected directly into someone's veins."

My hand flew to my throat and my eyes widened in horror at his words. "Poison ... oh my God!" I replied in a stricken voice barely above a whisper.

"Where are you now?" Allen asked on the other end of the line. I could hear the tension in his words.

"I'm with my friends Lionel and Lily in Charlottesville. Why?"

"Good. Don't go anywhere alone. Make sure you keep the doors locked on the house when you're home. I'm not trying to scare you but someone has already attempted to harm you once and now this. Just be on your guard."

"Do you think Grannie was poisoned in the same way?"

"It's possible. Without an autopsy, it's pure conjecture," Allen said. "Look, keep this information under your hat. I just wanted you to know so you'll be aware. Call me if you see or hear anything suspicious."

"Okay. Thank you." I ended the call and raised my eyes to my friends. "Did you hear what he said?"

"Yeah, I heard. Man ... antifreeze as a poison. Wicked stuff." Lionel spoke in a low voice, glancing over his shoulder, afraid we might be overheard.

"I'm sorry Maddie. I didn't believe you when you told me Grannie's death seemed suspicious, but now I think you're right. You started to tell us you knew who killed her when the phone rang. What were you going to say?" Lily asked. She reached across the table to clasp my hand.

The suspense built as Lily and Lionel focused their attention on me.

I nervously scanned the room before leaning forward to confide in my friends.

"It's got to be Wallace Jackson. Who else would gain by Grannie's death? He wants our property and I think he'd do anything, even murder, to get it."

"That's a serious accusation. But why would he need to kill Noah? We agree both deaths must be connected, right?" asked Lily.

"I dunno. Maybe Noah blackmailed him, or maybe Noah found something to incriminate him. Remember, I told you I saw Noah pick up an object in the barn. What if the needle he found contained poison used on Grannie? We were thinking it was drugs, but what if it wasn't? He told Sean he had found something profitable. It's the only thing that makes sense," I said, warming up to my theory.

I sat back in my chair and folded my arms across my chest. The more I thought about it, the more convinced I became I was right.

Lionel drew in a long breath, "I hate to throw cold water on your theory, but Wallace Jackson couldn't have killed Noah or your Grannie."

I sat forward in my chair and stared at him. "How do you know that?" I refused to believe otherwise.

"I've been digging into the background on that lien, like I told you. Attorney Warner asked me to track Jackson's movements and what I found out was that on the day your grandmother died, Jackson was in Richmond filing an appeal brief. Warner called his office yesterday to discuss the particulars of that lien. The secretary informed him that Jackson and his family were spending the week at their beach house on the Chesapeake. He's not expected back until next Wednesday. So he couldn't have done either murders; he's got solid alibis," Lionel explained.

My mind spun. I'd been so certain. If Jackson didn't do it, then who did? I was back at square one, trying to determine a suspect.

"I can't believe I was so wrong! However, just because he's got an alibi for the killing, doesn't let him off the hook for trying to steal my property. In my mind, he's guilty of that until I see solid proof otherwise. But where do we go from here? Who else would benefit from my grandmother's death and where does Noah fit into all of this?"

"Guess we keep digging. What about that kid, Sean? Is he still being held and questioned by the police?" asked Lionel.

"As far as I know, he is. But he's innocent. There's no way Sean could have killed my Grannie and I heard him tell Noah he didn't want any part of Noah's scheme. I just don't see him involved. He's a decent kid."

"Hate to say it," Lily spoke as she stabbed her fork into the salad, "but we're running out of suspects."

"Maybe. There's still one," I whispered as my mind shuddered to go there.

Chapter Nineteen

Hidden Passage

Chief Bill Barlow watched and listened to the interrogation of the Irish lad by detective Allen Crawford. It still rankled him that the upstart Philadelphia Yankee had stolen the detective position right out from under his nephew Ronnie. Of course Barlow didn't have any say in the matter when it was the police commissioner's decision to bring in the outsider. Dang, it sure made him mad, though.

The chief watched the kid squirm in his seat and stutter. Crawford kept drilling him; he'd give him that. He'd get an answer out of that boy soon.

"Tell me again what you were doing yesterday morning? Why were you in the barn?" demanded Crawford in a menacing voice as he paced the floor of the interview room and stopped next to Sean's chair.

"I told you; I was lookin' for Noah to tell him I was gonna go into town. That's all."

"Why did you look for him in the barn? Was Noah frequently in the barn?"

Sean fidgeted in his seat. He dragged his fingers through his disheveled red hair then looked squarely at the detective. "When I stood on the porch, I heard voices talking from the direction of the barn.

Noah and Bobbie Jo often met in the barn loft for a bit of a tryst, if you know what I mean, so I thought I'd find him there."

"Do you always need his permission to go into town?" needled Crawford.

"No sir. But it helps to get the keys to the truck and Noah had them in his pocket." Sean took a cleansing breath and leaned back in his seat.

"All right. So you went into the barn to get the keys to the truck. What happened next? Did you argue? Were you jealous about Noah's relationship with this girl?" Crawford kept pushing for answers.

Sean gave a half laugh. "Hardly! No offense to Miss Maddie, but her cousin is a bit of a slut. Pardon my saying so, but she's not someone I'd likely get jealous over."

Crawford coughed and covered his mouth with his hand to hide his grin as he raised his eyes to the two-way mirror and the Chief observing the session.

"So you heard voices ... were they in conversation, speaking low or raised voices in an argument? Tell me what you heard or saw. If you didn't jab Noah Foster with that needle, convince me of who did."

Perspiration beaded across Sean's forehead. He swiped his face with the hem of his t-shirt.

"Initially, the voices talked normal then they got louder, like in an argument. When I approached the barn door, suddenly the voices had stopped. I didn't hear anyone. The barn was dark after coming in out of the bright sunshine and at first I saw nothing amiss, until I almost tripped over Noah's feet. He was just laying there. I swear, I didn't touch him. The dog, Luke, was growling and barking at someone in the back of the barn. When Luke saw me, he charged, his teeth all bared and snarling. Frightened the heebie-jeebies out of me, I don't mind telling you. I ran into one of the empty stalls to climb the walls; that's where Luke cornered me. I was there when Miss Maddie and her handyman Tom entered the barn."

"Did you see anyone else?" the detective questioned.

"No, just Noah all crumpled like."

"Have you and Noah been friends a long time? Tell me about this profitable idea that he had."

That question caught Sean by surprise. His eyes widened and his jaw dropped. He almost fell off his seat as he jumped back.

Sean stuttered as he started to answer, then stopped and took a deep breath. "You've got the wrong idea, mate. I only just met Noah Foster at the beginning of the school year; we were assigned to room together. Noah had lots of ideas for getting rich quick but I told him I wanted no part of his wonky plans. You've got to believe me. I had no part in this scheme."

"You think about those voices you heard. Were they male or female? Give it some thought. I'll be right back," Crawford said as he picked up his folder and left the room.

"What do you think?" the detective asked his chief as he joined him. "Think he's telling the truth?"

"Well, you've been at it for four hours now and his story hasn't changed. You rattled him with that last point about the profitable scheme. His face turned as white as a ghost. He's going to wonder how you knew about that."

"Yeah, he definitely reacted to that. I dunno, Chief, I don't think he'd have enough time to fight with the victim and jab him with that needle before Tom Borden and Maddie Brooke came onto the scene. I'm leaning toward thinking the three of them all arrived minutes after the attack and after the perpetrator got away. The only one that got a close look at our perp was the dog."

"Hmm, I tend to agree. We can hold O'Reilly for twenty-four hours before we have to charge him; put him in a cell and let him sweat it out. Let's see if he confesses or we learn anything new."

"Okay, Chief. You got it."

Crawford walked back into the interrogation room. Sean sat hunched over the table, his head in his hands. He raised his head at the sound of the officer's approach.

"O'Reilly, you're going to be a guest of the county for a few more hours. Follow me."

"Are you arresting me?" asked Sean.

"Not yet. But you aren't free to leave just now either."

Crawford led the young Irishman down the corridor to a bank of holding cells and ushered him inside. The iron door clanged, a formidable and lonely sound, as it shut and locked behind him.

"Make yourself comfortable. A guard will deliver a dinner tray to you."

Sean nodded and collapsed onto the narrow cot. His face blanched, a portrait of fear and bewilderment. Crawford almost felt sorry for the young man.

I was alone at the inn. Tom had left for the day. I debated over what to eat for supper but wasn't in the mood. Since the Campbell family had checked out, I sought to savor the solitary peace of the farm while I could. Bobbie Jo had run off; I had no idea where. Lately, she disappeared often. Only Grannie's ghost and Luke provided company for me.

Detective Allen Crawford's black sedan crunched over the gravel as he pulled into the driveway of the Magnolia Blossom Inn. I watched him step out, adjusting his hat and straightening his suit coat. Dusk shrouded the yard in deep shadows, and a light breeze rustled the magnolia blossoms, carrying their sweet scent through the air. The sound of chickens clucking and pecking in the pen mingled with Prissy's meow and her kittens mewling.

I met him halfway, crossing my arms to keep from shaking with frustration. I'd been fretting all day, worrying about Sean while simultaneously trying to concentrate on the clues to Grannie's death and Noah's. I was in a foul temper.

"Detective Crawford, you're wasting your time. Sean O'Reilly didn't kill Noah Foster. When are you going to release him?" I spoke quickly with no greeting.

He sighed, looking tired. "Are we back to being formal? It's Allen, remember? I thought our relationship had progressed further than that. Sorry Maddie, but we've been through this already about Sean. He had motive and opportunity. We're holding him for questioning, that's all."

"Opportunity? Really?" I said, my voice rising. "Because he happened to be nearby? He was helping with the cherry festival and cherry picking that morning, and you know it."

Crawford shook his head, his expression stern. "There's a thirty-minute gap where his whereabouts are unaccounted for. And that syringe with the poison? We found a bottle of antifreeze hidden in his room when the team searched."

"Antifreeze in his room ... I didn't know that. But that doesn't mean it was his. Isn't it possible the real killer hid it there? Noah and Sean shared that room; maybe it belonged to Noah and not Sean." I snapped, my patience wearing thin. "Noah was involved in some dangerous stuff with that blackmail scheme. I told you I heard him talk about his plot. Sean was trying to stop him, not kill him."

Crawford raised an eyebrow. "Maddie, I understand you want to believe the best in people, but Sean had every reason to act desperate. Consider the facts: he needed money for school tuition plus he didn't have a job. Maybe he changed his mind and wanted in on Noah's plan but Noah refused."

"And that's why he would kill Noah?" I shot back. I shook my head then sighed loudly. "Noah must have had enemies, like whoever he was blackmailing. Did you consider that person might have done this?"

Crawford's eyes narrowed slightly as he considered my words. "We're looking into all possibilities, Maddie. But the evidence we have points to Sean."

I took a deep breath, trying to calm the storm brewing inside me. "While you waste your time questioning Sean, the actual killer is getting away. It just makes me see red! Okay then, let's go over it again. You want to search the barn and their room again? Fine. But I'm coming with you."

Allen nodded, agreeing to my suggestion, and we walked together toward the barn. Luke trotted along at my side. I left my crutches on the porch and limped along, careful to not put any strain on my tender ankle. The old wooden structure stood silently. Its weathered boards wore a myriad of colors in the waning evening light. The barn door creaked as Crawford pushed it open wider, and we stepped inside. Our movements stirred up the air as we entered the barn. Dust motes and wisps of straw floated in the disturbed air.

"Allen, you must see this for what it is," I said, my voice echoing slightly in the empty barn. "Sean wasn't here when my grandmother died. He had nothing to do with that. Yet I believe she was poisoned, too. Maybe the syringe that Noah found and that I saw him pocket had something to do with her death."

Crawford paused, his flashlight sweeping the dark corners. "It's possible, but we never confirmed that, Maddie. Her death simply could have been natural causes like Doctor Houser certified. I've got to go on facts."

I shook my head vehemently. "And then there's the attack on me. The one that left me with this sprained ankle. You said before that you don't believe in coincidences. The more I've thought about it, the more I agree with you. My injury, Grannie, and Noah's death are all connected. Allen, whoever is behind this madness must be trying to cover their tracks. What if he strikes again?"

Allen's eyes met mine. "We can't prove anything unless we find the missing link that ties both deaths together. How did our killer even escape out of this barn, for example?"

I nodded. "I understand, but Sean is just a convenient scapegoat. Whoever is behind this is still out there."

He looked thoughtful, then nodded. "Alright. Let's see if there's anything we missed."

We moved through the darkening barn methodically, searching for anything out of place. Prissy gathered her kittens to her protectively and meowed indignantly at our intrusion while Luke trotted behind me as we moved about the stalls. We found nothing out of the ordinary. Grannie's ghost hovered in the loft, observing our movements. She remained silent as I crawled about the barn stalls and poked among the tools and equipment hanging on the wooden walls.

I paused and stood up, stretching my back. Brushing my hair out of my face, I turned to the detective. "You know, I suspected our family lawyer, Wallace Jackson. I was positive he killed Grannie and plotted to steal our land. I admit it, I just couldn't see anyone else guilty except him. Just like how you feel about Sean. But I was wrong and you'll see you are too."

Allen looked at me incredulously. "Why would you think an attorney would be involved?"

"Well, because he kept prodding Grannie and then me to sell the inn and land. He was acting awfully suspicious. I even found him poking around in here one day."

"Maybe my office should investigate him. How do you know you're wrong?" Allen asked.

"No. Don't bother. My friend Lionel already checked out his alibis and Jackson was out of town during both murders."

The detective snorted as he stared at me in wonder. "Just who is this Lionel?"

"Um, like I said, he's a friend of mine. You met him once. Lionel works at the African-American Heritage Center in Charlottesville. He's an I.T. specialist. He checked on Jackson and said he was in Richmond when Grannie died and also out of town with his family at the beach when Noah died. So he's out of the picture."

This time, Allen did laugh out loud. "Well, guess you can thank Lionel for me. Tell him I appreciate him doing my job but perhaps he better leave the investigation to the police in the future."

My lips curled into a pout. "He was only trying to help. Honestly, he wouldn't have done that without my insistence. Lionel's investigation proved the debt on my deed was false. We're planning on going after Jackson for fraud."

"Oh yeah? What debt and who's we?"

"Me and Attorney Lee Warner from the Center. He's the legal counsel there and it's his office that is researching the false fifty-thousand dollar lien on my deed."

"Hmm. That's a lot of money. So he thinks you have a case, huh?"

"Yes he does. Getting out from under that huge debt, is a major relief. Of course, I was more concerned about learning who killed Grannie and Noah. I'm afraid we aren't any closer to solving that problem."

"Well, let's keeping looking. There's got to be some clue left behind or over looked."

Allen and I continued our search. Eventually, we stood at the back of the barn and gazed forward. The wide double doors gaped open in front of us; above our heads, the loft stretched across half the width of the barn with a shuttered window in the loft's front. Only one entrance in and one way out both at the front of the barn. The mystery revolved around both the how, and the who, could have killed two individuals.

Running from the corner of the barn, Luke barked and ran back and forth, as if trying to communicate with us.

"What is it boy?" I asked Luke.

He barked again and wagged his tail then shook his head.

"Maybe something's back here," I suggested to Allen as we moved into the rear corner of the barn.

"Probably just a mouse or one of those kittens," remarked Allen.

A short stack of hay bales were piled in the corner. Allen stepped around the bales. As he leaned against the bales scanning the expanse of the barn, he braced himself with a hand on the wooden wall at the rear corner. One of the wooden planks moved. It swung outward as if hinged. Allen lost his balance and stumbled forward, catching himself on the bales.

I gasped, "Oh my goodness!"

"Well, well. We may have found our killer's exit route." Stooping, Allen crawled through the opening then stood up. Studying his surroundings, he called to me, "Come on out."

I crawled through the open panel with Luke squeezing through right behind me. I found myself behind the henhouse attached perpendicular to the side of the barn; its angled position blocked my view of the house. I stood in a protected L-shaped alcove. When I turned around, rows of leafy apple trees in the orchard filled the horizon. It would be so easy for someone to come and go unobserved.

My face mirrored my surprise. "I never knew that panel opened. That's got to be how the killer entered and exited the barn without being seen."

"I believe you may be right. If Sean O'Reilly had known about the hidden door, he would have used it instead of running toward the front and being attacked by Luke. I may be able to release him because of this but I still want to search his room again to be sure."

Luke barked then trotted ahead of us in the dark, leading us around the perimeter of the henhouse and back into the main graveled yard. We faced the open barn doors with the chicken coop to its left.

Heading back into the house, we went up to room number five at the end of the hall previously shared by Sean and Noah. The room was neat but showed signs of a previous methodical search.

Crawford started going through drawers and closets again, and I watched, feeling a mixture of hope and anxiety. "Look," I said, pointing to a stack of notebooks and a laptop on the desk. "Noah's journals and his computer. Maybe there's something in there."

The detective flipped open the top book, skimming the pages. "My office checked these once. I'll need to take them in for a closer look. They might have some clues but I doubt it. I don't think he'd be stupid enough to write anything down that would incriminate himself."

I nodded, relieved he was finally considering other possibilities. "And what about Noah's laptop and Sean's tablet?"

Crawford sighed. "We'll dig into them again. If I find anything suspicious in either search engines or history, I'll let you know."

I took a deep breath, feeling a little lighter. "Thank you, Allen. For keeping an open mind."

He gave me a small, tired smile. "Don't thank me yet, Maddie. We still have a lot of work to do."

"If you need any help with that laptop or the tablet, I could ask my friend Lionel."

He turned to me with a raised eyebrow and a frown, "Just how close of a friend is this Lionel?"

I blushed prettily and batted my eyelashes in an exaggerated manner that made him laugh. In a honey sweet voice I declared, "Why detective! Just what aaaare you implying? Are you jealous?"

"Hardly. But, uh, a guy's gotta know what his competition is." He waggled his eyebrows.

Now it was my turn to laugh. "You don't have to worry about Lionel. If anything, I'm the one who has to be concerned about the competition, if you get my drift."

"Oh! I get you." A light blush colored his cheeks.

As Allen left, I felt a renewed sense of determination. There was still so much to uncover, but I knew one thing for sure: Sean was innocent. I would do everything in my power to unearth who did murder Noah and my beloved Grannie. It couldn't be Sean and Lionel had ruled out Wallace Jackson, so who else had a motive? My mind kept coming back to those burnt love letters. Time to question Grannie about the identity of the author; she'd been silent too long. The solution to this mystery seemed tied to the past. It was worth another look at family records and photos to uncover the link.

Chapter Twenty

Unraveling Secrets

The next day, I waited anxiously for a call from the police station and the release of Sean. Allen had promised he'd let the man go. My foot felt sufficiently healed to be able to drive our truck; I only needed the go ahead to pick him up. Eggs collected, animals fed, and morning chores completed— still no word from Allen.

Late afternoon sun bathed the Magnolia Blossom Inn in a warm, golden light, casting long shadows across the front yard. Bees buzzing in the garden blooms created a low hum. A breeze carried the sweet fragrance of magnolia blossoms mixed with honeysuckle. The balmy blend did little to calm my nerves. I needed to stay busy while I waited.

Sitting on the front porch, I opened the box of documents and photographs at my feet. Sorting the older black and white snapshots, I put them aside and concentrated on the papers. After hours of finding only paid receipts and feed bills, I gave up. I had hoped to learn more family history that could provide a clue to our current mystery. Maybe there was another way.

The weight of my thoughts pressed heavily on my shoulders. Leaning back against the rocker, I looked toward the heavens and took a deep breath. A plan of sorts sprung to my mind.

Doctor Houser's behavior had been gnawing at me ever since Grannie's death. There were too many unanswered questions, too many suspicious coincidences. I phoned his office and asked him to stop by on the ruse of checking my ankle. It was time to confront him and get to the bottom of this.

"Yes, Maddie, I can stop by. As a matter of fact, I wanted to talk to you. I spoke with Detective Crawford and he informed me about the ethylene glycol poison in that syringe. There's something you should know," Doctor Houser said in a hesitant voice.

"I'll see you soon then." And now I waited. My eyes closed as I dozed off in the heat of the late afternoon.

Luke barked in his alert voice. Startled, I hurried across the wraparound porch to the back side of the house and kitchen door. I found Luke pawing at the screen door; someone had shut the inside door and the dog couldn't get in. The doctor's car was parked in the rear. Funny, I didn't hear him drive up or see him enter the house. When did he get here? Where was he?

With a determined breath, I walked back into the house. The familiar scent of beeswax and old wood filled the air, a comforting reminder of the years of history contained within these walls. As I made my way through the inn, the creak of the floorboards beneath my feet seemed louder than usual, echoing in the silence and raising my apprehension.

"Doctor Houser?" I called. My voice shook slightly. He had to be here.

"Maddie?" His voice came from the study. "I'm in here," he said with a hint of embarrassment in his tone.

I found him sitting at Grannie's old writing desk, leafing through the additional family photographs and papers I had left there last night.

His face softened when he saw me, but something flickered—guilt or worry perhaps?—in his eyes.

"We need to talk," I said, stepping into the room and closing the door behind me.

He set the pictures aside. "I wandered in here looking for you. I apologize for invading your privacy but I couldn't help myself when I saw the photographs. She was so lovely," he said wistfully. His fingers caressed a picture of Grannie.

Shaking my head, I took a deep breath, my heart pounding. Now that I faced him, my courage fled. "I don't mind about the pictures. Um, I want to know the truth about why you were always on the scene and so quickly every time a death occurred."

The doctor's expression grew serious. "I don't understand. What are you getting at?"

I walked closer, feeling a surge of determination. "Like how you were suddenly on the scene when Grannie died and johnnie- on-the-spot before the paramedics got here when Noah died. I can't help wondering if you were in that barn because you did the killing."

There I said it! Shock at my own blurted words colored my face. My common sense had completely abandoned my brain. What was I thinking to risk confronting a potential murderer?

His face paled, and he leaned back in his chair, running a hand through his graying hair.

"I told you I had simply listened to my police scanner and that helped me arrive quickly. I confess, I often used the scanner to arrive on the scene before other medical personnel. I needed the money. I'm just a small country doctor and my practice is shrinking even smaller. Arriving first gave me a chance to bill a patient I might not have had." He wrung his hands and shifted his gaze away from me.

I shook my head in disbelief. "You're an ambulance chaser?" My accusation embarrassed him as he turned pleading eyes to me.

"Maddie, I would never harm Polly. She was a dear friend. I took an oath to help people and do no harm. I couldn't kill anyone. You're way off base."

His words registered with me. Pouncing on one key statement, I studied his expression. "A friend? Or something more?"

He sighed, lowering his gaze to his hands. "It's true. I've loved Polly since we were young. I wanted to marry her, but she chose Charles Brooke, and I respected that."

I blinked, taken aback by his candid confession. "You loved her?"

"Yes," he whispered. "And she knew it. But she didn't feel the same way. She loved Charles."

I took a seat across from him, trying to process this new information. "Wilbur Houser. It was your initial *W* on those love letters. Grannie told me to burn them after she died."

His eyes widened in realization. "She kept those letters?"

"Yes," I replied. "She told me they were from an old admirer. Was that you?"

He nodded slowly. "I wrote those letters many years ago when I asked her to marry me. They were a way for me to express my feelings, knowing she would never return the same emotion."

I felt a pang of guilt for suspecting him, but I had to know more. "Doctor Houser, you must understand why I'm suspicious. Grannie's death, Noah's murder ... it all seems connected somehow."

He shook his head, his eyes filled with sorrow. "Maddie, I would never harm Polly. I loved her too much. I didn't know that kid Noah. But I remembered something about Bobbie Jo that I wanted to tell you. Maybe that detective should know that Bobbie Jo worked as a candy striper at the hospital one summer."

I searched his face for any sign of deceit but found only earnest sincerity. A heavy silence settled between us as I tried to absorb his words. It seemed I had misjudged Doctor Houser, but I still felt like I was missing something.

"Maybe I better phone Allen, I mean Detective Crawford, and tell him what you said. It might be important." I pulled my cell phone out of my pocket and called the private number Allen had given me. He answered after the second ring.

"Hello, Maddie? What's wrong?"

"Allen. Doctor Houser is here and he told me—" My voice caught in my throat as the floorboards creaked and the study door flew open. I dropped my phone onto the desktop.

Bobbie Jo stepped into the room, her face set in a tight smile. "What's going on in here?"

I stiffened, my instincts on high alert. "Just having a chat with Doctor Houser. He was telling me you used to work as a candy striper in the hospital. I should have known by the precise hospital corners you made on the bed sheets. Guess that's when you learned how to handle a hypodermic needle." I challenged her with a look.

Bobbie Jo's smile widened, but it didn't reach her eyes. "Yeah, what of it? Oh, Maddie, always digging for secrets. Be careful what you find. You might not be able to handle it."

I frowned, sensing an edge to her words. "What do you mean by that?"

She shrugged, her gaze drifted to the pictures and letters on the desk. "Secrets can hurt people, Maddie. Maybe it's best to let the past stay in the past."

Doctor Houser looked uncomfortable, glancing between us. "Bobbie Jo, Maddie is just trying to understand what happened to Polly and Noah. We all are."

Bobbie Jo's eyes flickered with something dark and unreadable. "Well, sometimes understanding comes at a price."

The tension in the room was palpable. I felt an icy chill run down my spine with a sudden, inexplicable urge to escape the study. Before I could act on it, Bobbie Jo moved closer, her expression hardening. She picked up a vase and crashed it down on the doctor's head. The elderly man slumped onto the desk. His injured head dripped blood onto the desk blotter.

A scream escaped from my mouth as I jumped off my chair and

grabbed a box of tissues. I moved toward the unconscious man intending to staunch his bleeding but Bobbie Jo blocked me.

"Let me near him. He needs help!" I cried.

"I don't care about that old man. He needs to keep his mouth shut and not meddle where he doesn't belong," she sneered as she advanced on me, shoving me backwards. "You know, Maddie," she said, her voice low and threatening, "some people don't deserve what they have. They don't appreciate it. And sometimes, it takes a little push to set things right."

Her hands on my chest, she pushed me harder, causing me to stumble again.

My heart pounded in my chest as I realized the genuine danger I faced. "Bobbie Jo, what are you talking about?"

She laughed, a high, almost manic sound. "You're so blind, Maddie. Yes, I killed Grannie. I poisoned her because this property should have been mine. It was always supposed to be mine."

I took a step back, fear gripping me. "You ... you killed Grannie?" Why didn't I see her possessiveness sooner? I should have found some clue in those family records. What did I miss when researching the family tree? It was no good second-guessing myself now.

"Yes," she hissed, her eyes wild. "I came to talk to her about my share of the inn and she laughed at me. But I fixed her. All it took was one little needle prick in her neck's carotid artery. I heard you coming. I had to throw the syringe away. Didn't have time to hide it before that damn dog pounced on me too."

"What about Noah? Did you kill him too?" I asked. I backed away from her as I spotted my cell phone partially covered by one of the black and white pictures. The call line was still open. I prayed Allen was listening.

"Noah thought he had found a gold mine. Stupid fool tried to blackmail me with that poisoned syringe he found. So I had to silence him too. And now, I have to deal with you."

Suddenly, she pulled a butcher knife from behind her back. The blade gleamed in the dim light. I inched backward, seeking an escape, but became pressed against the window.

"Bobbie Jo. Don't do this," I pleaded, trying to keep my voice steady. My eyes searched for something, anything, within reach to defend myself. Nothing.

She advanced on me; the knife raised. "It's too late, Maddie. This is my birthright. My legacy. You don't deserve any of it."

Grabbing the heavy window draperies, I yanked the fabric off its hooks and tossed it into Bobbie Jo's face. She flailed under the heavy weight.

In a desperate bid for safety, I turned and ran toward the door. Bobbie Jo recovered and threw off the drapery. She caught my arm and yanked me back. The knife flashed dangerously close to my face. I struggled, but my tender ankle threatened to give way.

Suddenly, a cold breeze swept through the room, and a faint, shimmering light appeared before Bobbie Jo. Grannie's ghost, her translucent form radiating an eerie glow, stared at Bobbie Jo with fierce, protective eyes.

"Bobbie Jo," Grannie's voice threatened in a loud command. *"This madness ends now."* Grannie's body materialized into a solid form as she inserted herself between Bobbie Jo and me.

Bobbie Jo's eyes widened in terror as she stared in horror at the apparition. She stepped back; her face contorted. "No ... no, you can't be real!"

Grannie's ghost moved closer, menacing, her presence growing stronger. *"You will not harm Maddie. You won't hurt anyone again or I'll see you in hell."*

With a shriek, Bobbie Jo tripped backward, losing her balance. She toppled over a chair. The knife clattered to the floor. I scrambled to my feet, kicked the knife away, and rushed to the other side of the room.

At that moment, the study door burst open. Detective Allen Crawford, his gun drawn, and two officers stormed in. Luke, gaining access to the house, barked furiously by his side. Allen took in the scene; his eyes widened as he saw Bobbie Jo sprawled on the floor, sobbing hysterically. He glanced toward Doctor Houser moaning and struggling to raise his head from the desk top.

"Maddie are you alright?" he asked, rushing to my side.

I nodded; tears streamed down my face in relief. "She ... she tried to kill me. And she killed Grannie and Noah."

"I know. I heard it all over your phone. We've got her confession recorded."

Crawford's face hardened as he cuffed Bobbie Jo, who was too stunned and terrified to resist. "You're under arrest for the murders of Polly Brooke and Noah Foster."

As Crawford led Bobbie Jo out of the room, I rushed to the doctor's side and applied a wad of tissue to the cut on his head. The bleeding had decreased and clotted.

Doctor Houser's face was pale but recovering. "Maddie, I'm so sorry. I should have said something earlier."

I shook my head, trying to process everything that had just happened. "It's not your fault, Doctor Houser. I'm sorry I suspected you. Let's get you some medical help. Can you stand?"

He gave me a small, reassuring smile. "I'll be okay. You can't hurt this old hard head."

I glanced back at the spot where Grannie's ghost had appeared. I thought of the love cherished by a man for the girl of his youth. And the love shared between a grandmother and granddaughter that death could not break—both greater than any ancient festering hatred. The air was warm again; the light gone. But I knew Grannie was still with me, watching over me.

Allen returned; his eyes reflected his concern and perhaps a deeper emotion. "Maddie, you were very brave. We'll make sure Bobbie Jo pays for what she's done."

I nodded, still in shock. "Thanks Allen. I don't know what I would have done if you hadn't shown up in time. Bobbie Jo needs help; she's mentally ill. I realize now she'd become insanely obsessed with her claims of inheritance. I just wish I had recognized it earlier. All my historical research, yet I never uncovered the link that joined our families. Makes me feel foolish." I shook my head, sadly recalling my cousin being led away in handcuffs.

"Greed ... Bobbie Jo wanted it all. She craved the wealth and position that she thought owning this land would give her," Allen voiced his thoughts. "I've seen it before. Money corrupts."

"Humph, if she only knew ... owning this place is more hard work and debt than monetary wealth. The real fortune lays in the history and knowledge of this place and the people who came before us. Bobbie Jo didn't understand that," I mused.

Luke trotted over; his tail wagged as he nudged my hand with his nose. I scratched his ears, grateful for his comforting presence.

"Good boy, Luke. You tried to get in to save me but you couldn't. First thing tomorrow, we cut a hinged doggie door into that back door." I kissed the top of his head and rubbed his muzzle.

I strolled out to the front porch and watched the paramedics finish tending to Wilbur Houser's head wound. The doctor appeared to be a cooperative patient, appreciative of their administrations. Sitting on the porch swing, I leaned my head back and breathed in the country air. Grateful the nightmare was over.

Allen joined me on the porch as a pair of officers placed a dazed Bobbie Jo into the back seat of a police cruiser. A team of policemen snapped pictures in the crime scene. I smiled invitingly at Allen as he joined me on the swing.

"I, uh, have to ask. When you were fighting with your cousin, I thought I heard another voice through the phone. Who was that? I listened closely but my phone crackled for a few seconds blocking the sound then it seemed to clear when I heard your voice again. Do you know what that was?"

"Hmm, no, I can't say what that was. You saw for yourself only the three of us occupied the study and poor Doctor Houser was out cold. Must have been static. I wouldn't worry about it."

Epilogue

In the days that followed, the truth about Bobbie Jo's crimes came to light. She had been driven by a twisted sense of entitlement, believing that the Magnolia Blossom Inn and lands rightfully belonged to her because of her ancestry. Back in 1865, Camilla Lord had married Thomas Brooke. The Lord descendants through various marriages populated Bobbie Jo's family tree. It was what made Maddie's mother, Eleanor, a distant third cousin to Bobbie Jo's mother. This connection made Bobbie Jo think she deserved more rights to the property than Maddie. She didn't consider Maddie's direct line of ascension through her father and the Brooke heirs.

Bobbie Jo's obsession had led her to commit the unthinkable, and she now faced the consequences of her actions.

Detective Crawford and his team uncovered the full extent of Noah's blackmail scheme and how Bobbie Jo had silenced him to protect her dark secret. The district attorney ultimately indicted Bobbie Jo on two counts of first degree murder, and one count of attempted murder, plus assault.

Attorney Lee Warner filed fraud charges on behalf of the Magnolia Blossom Inn and farm against Esquire Wallace Jackson in civil court, citing the shell corporations and false lien claimed against the Brooke property. The judge dismissed the lien. The court suspended Jackson for a one-year period of time, plus charged him a penalty fine of ten thousand dollars payable to the plaintiff for the perpetrated fraud. Maddie donated half of the award to the Heritage Center in Charlottesville.

The revelations in both murder cases, as well as, the fraud committed by their local attorney, shocked the citizens of Clarkstown. Elvira Ginther's mouth gaped open, considering the scandal. Ultimately, a sense of relief that justice had been served settled on the town.

With Bobbie Jo in custody, I finally relaxed. Life gradually returned to normal. Sean returned to the inn but resided only long enough until he could arrange a transfer of his school records back to Dublin. He planned to return to Ireland to finish his education and live with his family.

Poor Doctor Houser suffered a headache for days, but as he said, his hard head would heal. Luke still growls whenever he sees the man and it was only recently that I learned why. Grannie had once asked the doctor to administer Luke's immunization shots one time as a favor to her instead of using the vet. Now Luke remembers and suspects the doctor will jab him with a painful needle whenever he comes near.

Lionel and Lily continued to offer me their support and friendship as we planned a celebration party at the inn. I looked forward to the upcoming event as I scribbled notes for a menu while seated at the kitchen table.

The inn grew busier than ever with the newly improved website. We booked reservations for the balance of the summer and the beginning of the fall tourism season. I placed an ad to hire a full-time housekeeper now that the inn was on a solid financial footing; interviews were booked for tomorrow.

A light breeze and waft of cold air circulated in the room. I looked up from my party list as Grannie joined me.

"You did it, Maddie. You protected Magnolia Blossom Inn and your inheritance. The Brooke family land is safe."

"Did I ever thank you for saving my life?" I asked her, recalling how she defended me from Bobbie Jo's attack.

"I told you I'd look after you. My sweet baby girl ... no one will harm you if I can help it."

I voiced what had been on my mind since the incident. "Grannie, now that you know how you died, I suppose this means you can leave? Go on into the light, as they say?" I would miss her terribly, but I'll always cherish the comforting knowledge that love transcends even death.

"Yes, I could. But I rather like it here. I think I'll stick around." Grannie's laugh rang out as she vanished. Luke barked and jumped up and down, trying to catch the ethereal bubble that floated away.

About the Author

Now an award winning author, Nancy M. Wade challenged herself to finish the novel that had been started years earlier after she retired from the Dept. of Defense in 2012. The result one year later was "Endless Circle: A Circle D Saga".

Nancy and her husband are living their retirement dream in the hills of N.E. Tennessee. She's an active member of the Lost State Writer's Guild of the Tri-Cities area of TN/VA. Determined to complete another personal challenge and bucket list item, Nancy went back to school at the golden age of 69 to complete her bachelor's degree. Graduating in 2022 with Summa Cum Laude honors from East State Tennessee University, Nancy concentrated in criminology and film studies.

An avid lover of western movies and books, Nancy developed the Circle-D Saga — a western action adventure tale of love and hatred. The story begins in "Endless Circle" with generations of three families: the Dunlap, Logan, and Hartman families. The saga follows the families during WWII in "Moment in Time" and the 3rd book in the trilogy called "Gun for Hire" tells the tale of gunslinger Cody Jarvis and his connection to the dynasty.

Based upon her years of living in the mid-west, Nancy wrote a small town, cozy mystery series: "A Meadowood Mystery", with the antics of amateur sleuth housewife, Meredith Gardner, in "Scarecrows and Corpses", then added more adventures in "Reunion with Death", "Deadly Bones", "Deathly Wedding Woes", and the holiday tale "Berry Little Murder".

She is also the author of a rich family drama, _Reflections: A Sentimental Journey_ inspired by the courtship and early married years of her parents;_a colonial historical romance novel, _Frontier Heart_; and a contemporary short story called _Courtship of Laura._

Follow Nancy's upcoming projects on her web site: https://nancymwadeauthor.com and on her social media links.

www.ingramcontent.com/pod-product-compliance
Lightning Source LLC
Chambersburg PA
CBHW060459300726
48975CB00008B/2569